ANIMAL INVESTIGATORS

WOLF MAN

Wolf Man stood between the injured Storm and his half-crazed attacker. It was an insane thing to do, in Meriel's opinion.

Meriel couldn't mind-read humans. But she could guess what Wolf Man was thinking. She could guess at his strong beliefs. He was telling himself, This wolf will back down. Wolves don't attack people.

Meriel couldn't help wondering what the lone wolf was thinking. But this was no time to go into a trance.

Besides, she could see, without mind-reading, that this was no ordinary wolf.

For more adventures from the

ANIMAL INVESTIGATORS

read:

RED EYE

GHOST DOGS

KILLER SPIDERS

ANIMAL INVESTIGATORS

WOLF MAN

S.P. GATES

USBORNE

First published in the UK in 2009 by Usborne Publishing Ltd.,
Usborne House, 83–85 Saffron Hill, London EC1N 8RT, England.
www.usborne.com

This is a work of fiction. The characters, incidents, and dialogues are
products of the author's imagination and are not to be construed as real.
Any resemblance to actual events or persons, living or dead, is entirely
coincidental.

A CIP catalogue record for this book is available from the British Library.

JFMAMJ ASOND/09   92036   ISBN 9780746097410
Printed in Great Britain.

CHAPTER ONE

The boy stumbled up the snow-covered mountain. There were men chasing him with weapons: spears, axes and bows and arrows. The men were howling, "Kill him! Kill him!"

The boy was the slave of a mighty shaman. He'd just stolen something from his master – the shaman's most feared and potent magic. And now the shaman's warriors were pursuing him to get it back.

The boy had been discovered, just as he made his escape. A warrior had bawled out, "Stop, thief!" The shaman himself had roared, "Hunt the slave down! Get back what is mine!"

It was bitter winter. The warriors chased the slave across a frozen lake, murder in their eyes. On the lower slopes of the mountain, the slave turned to fight. He was covered with the swirling blue tattoos of the tribe from which he'd been captured. Like all his tribe, he was a skilled archer. And he'd made his yew bow himself, and his arrows, flighted with goose feathers.

From behind a rock, he let an arrow fly. A warrior cried out, clutched his chest and fell. As the others took cover, the boy raced out from behind his rock. He tore the wolfskin cloak from the fallen warrior's body and snatched the axe from his hand. The slave boy had always wanted a wolfskin cloak and a fine copper axe. He slung the cloak round his shoulders.

The boy should have run then. But he didn't. Because, at the last moment, he noticed the fallen warrior had a dagger stuck into his belt, with a handle carved from mammoth tusk. The boy had always wanted one of those too.

He wasted precious seconds stooping to get it, sliding it inside his own belt. He didn't see the warrior who'd broken cover and was creeping up behind to ambush him...

Suddenly, the warrior leaped up and loosed an arrow. He yelled in triumph as it went whistling into the slave's back, through the wolfskin cloak. The slave staggered and nearly fell.

The slave turned and ran, slipping on icy rocks, plunging through deeper and deeper snowdrifts, with the men shrieking behind him.

At last, he turned to listen. His heart clenched with horror. Was that howling he heard?

It's only the wind, he decided.

He couldn't hear the shrieks of the warriors now. Had they given up the chase? The slave boy kept climbing, using the copper axe blade to chip handholds, footholds in the ice. He knew there was a cave higher up where he could shelter for the night. When dawn came, he'd go on, to his tribe beyond the mountains.

Will there be bears in the cave? he wondered. In his present state, he'd be too weak to fight them.

In spite of his desperate situation, the wounded boy gave a grim smile. Using his magic, the shaman had terrorized the whole land. No one could kill the shaman – his magic protected him. He led his warriors on night-time raids. They burned villages and kept the people as slaves. The boy's parents had been killed trying to save him and the boy himself taken captive.

But now I've taken the shaman's magic, thought the boy. *So he has no power any more.*

But had he lost any of the magic, during his mad scramble to get away?

He opened the leather pouch on his belt to check. It was packed with moss. Hidden inside it were the seven seeds he'd just taken. They were the shaman's secret, the source of his power. The slave boy breathed a sigh of relief. The seven seeds were still safe, undamaged. He could hardly believe such tiny things contained such potent magic, stronger by far than the magic of the wolf cloaks the shaman's warriors wore.

With clumsy, shaking fingers he tipped the seeds out onto his palm. They were glossy black with a scaly coating. Each had six sharp spikes, like tiny daggers. As soon as they touched his flesh, he felt a hot tingle shoot up his arm.

We are powerful, the seeds seemed to be telling him. *And all our power could be yours.*

"Destroy the magic!" the boy urged himself. Grind the seeds to powder with rocks, so they couldn't be used again by the shaman, or anyone else, to bring terror and death. "Do it now!" he ordered himself. "You must!"

But, somehow, he just couldn't. Already, the shaman's magic was starting to corrupt him. As it could most men and boys, even the bravest and noblest.

With freezing fingers, the slave boy hid the seeds again under the moss. He tied up the pouch, then stumbled on through a swirling blizzard.

He felt no pain from his arrow wound. The cold had numbed his whole body, right through to his bones. His feet, in his goatskin shoes, felt like heavy rocks. It was harder and harder to drag them. Soon he forgot about reaching the cave.

He just thought, *I must lie down and sleep.*

He curled up in the snow, still holding his axe. He wrapped the wolfskin cloak tightly around himself and closed his eyes. He imagined himself using the shaman's magic.

It made him mighty; no man could defeat him. He was so swift their arrows couldn't catch him, so savage they scattered before him. Terrible things had been done to him – his family had been slaughtered; he'd been made a slave. And he would do terrible things in his turn. He would take vengeance. People would be made to suffer, just as he had. Perhaps that would ease the bitter anger and pain he felt, deep inside.

His freezing fingers felt for the plaited leather band on his wrist. He had worn it throughout all his troubles. His father had made it, from the skin of the first deer the boy had hunted and killed.

The boy snuggled deeper into the snow, his head full of violent and bloodthirsty dreams. He didn't move again. Soon, his smile was a frozen mask, his eyelashes fringes of ice crystals. The hand grasping the axe froze solid. Gradually snow covered his whole body, first a light crust, then a blanket, then a drift many metres deep.

Many times the shaman's warriors came searching for him. But they never found him, or the seven seeds he'd stolen. Without his magic, the shaman's power was broken. His warriors left him. Finally, one day the shaman himself fled and was never seen again.

No trace of the boy was ever found. But his memory didn't die. His story was told to children around village fires – how a humble slave boy had defeated a mighty shaman by stealing his magic seeds. There were two versions of this story. One said that the boy had destroyed the shaman's seeds, for the good of all. But the other claimed that, like so many other men and boys before him, he'd been corrupted by their evil power and kept them for himself.

Both versions were passed on, down the generations.

As the years passed, the snow over the slave boy's body froze. Then a glacier flowed above his corpse, crushing it with its weight, burying it still deeper.

Centuries went by. In some remote places a few people still told stories about the slave boy and the shaman's magic seeds. But no one believed they were true any more. They belonged to the world of fairy tales.

ANIMAL INVESTIGATORS

Five thousand years passed and still the boy's body lay undiscovered, locked in its icy tomb. Until, in the twenty-first century, the glacier started to melt...

CHAPTER TWO

Ellis was teaching tracking at Wolf Camp to earn himself extra cash in his summer holidays. He'd got the job because Dr. Scott Spenser, who ran Wolf Camp, knew Professor Talltrees, Ellis's guardian.

Ellis was standing quietly behind a crowd of boys in a log cabin. Some were younger than him, still in junior school. A few were older. All of them were listening to Dr. Spenser welcome them to Wolf

Camp. Ellis's eyes were lowered. He seemed to be staring at the ground. But, secretly, he was checking the shoes that everyone wore, even Dr. Scott Spenser's. You never knew when information like that might come in useful.

"Hi, new Wolf Campers!" Scott Spenser greeted the new arrivals. "Now the first thing you need to know is: 'Don't be scared of wolves!' Wolves have a terrible reputation. Big bad wolves! That's how people see them. Think of *Little Red Riding Hood*! But wolves hardly ever attack people. If they saw you coming they'd vanish into the trees!"

Ellis's mind drifted away. He already knew all he needed to know about wolves. Instead, he thought about Meriel. Like him, she was a ward of Professor Talltrees. Together, the three of them made a formidable team, investigating animal mysteries.

Where are you, Meriel? wondered Ellis.

Ellis was a tracker, trained in Africa by a master tracker named Gift. Ellis's skills often seemed magical to people. But it was just a question of years of practice, of noticing details, picking up clues. But Meriel had a skill that was truly unique. She had the power to read the minds of wild creatures.

Meriel was half-wild herself, tricky to deal with and unpredictable. To Ellis's surprise she'd announced this morning, "I'm coming with you to Wolf Camp." But she'd slipped away from him at the entrance, off on some private business of her own, with Travis, her weasel friend, draped round her neck like a red scarf.

Meriel had been getting really restless lately. "We need a mission," Ellis had told her. Nothing interesting had happened for several weeks.

Except, Ellis reminded himself, something quite interesting was happening later today, back at the Natural History Museum, where they lived with Professor Talltrees. A body was being flown in by helicopter. It was a boy who'd been found up a mountain, frozen solid. Already, scientists had nicknamed him Tattooed Boy, because of the strange, swirling blue patterns that covered his body.

The Prof was really excited about it. "The Tattooed Boy's been in the ice since prehistoric times," he'd told his wards. "Five thousand years! And he was found with all his possessions. A copper axe, a dagger, a bow and arrows. It's fascinating!"

Ellis's mind snapped back to the present.

"So, Wolf Campers!" Scott was summing up. "What have we learned today? We've learned that wolves *aren't* the savage creatures of fairy tales. That they *aren't* dangerous to humans. They're probably more civilized than we are! So let's salute them with a great big wolf howl!"

Scott threw back his head and gave a long, soulful yowl. *"Oww, oww, oww!"*

From somewhere outside the log cabin came a thin, eerie howl in reply. Ellis felt the hairs prickle on the back of his neck. The howl came from the wolf enclosure, beyond the log cabins where the boys slept. The wolf enclosure was a big wood, eight kilometres square, surrounded by a high, spiked fence. Inside it was a wolf pack, running free. Ellis hadn't been in there yet; he'd only peered through the fence. And he hadn't seen any wolves. But like Scott had just said, wolves are very wary of humans. *Which isn't surprising*, thought Ellis, *considering that, in the past, humans have shot, gassed and trapped them, hunted them down with dogs, and almost made them extinct.*

"And again, kids," cried Scott. "Let's hear it for wolves!"

Some of the younger boys howled along with him, letting rip like they were real wolves. But some looked at Scott like he was a complete idiot. Others were clowning around, ignoring him completely.

Ellis cringed inside. Scott was a nice guy. He rarely got mad or shouted. He was always bubbling with enthusiasm. He was an expert in wolf lore. And he really cared about other people, especially the boys who came to Wolf Camp. *But he shouldn't go talking to them like they're five year olds,* thought Ellis.

Especially not these boys. They hadn't come to Wolf Camp voluntarily. They'd all been sent here because of antisocial behaviour. Scott was convinced they could learn lessons from wolves, about how to respect others, how to control their anger and aggression.

One of the older boys said, "I'm sick of all this talking. When do we get to meet the wolves?"

Ellis's gaze swung to the boy who'd asked the question. *He's trouble*, thought Ellis, immediately. A tracker like Ellis saw details others missed. He saw how the Wolf Campers had shuffled away from the boy who'd spoken, anxious not to invade his space.

How they watched him with sly, sideways glances as if they daren't make eye contact.

The boy had a half-starved look. He had spiky black hair. His thin face was white and pinched, like a mean old man's. His eyes were troubled. But they met Scott's with a defiant and scornful stare.

"I want you to shut up," he told Scott, "and take me to meet a wolf."

Scott ignored the boy's rudeness. "Your name's Nathan, isn't it?" he asked, still in the same friendly voice. "Do your mates call you Nate for short?"

"Not if they want to live," said Nathan.

A twitchy, red-haired boy hooted with laughter.

"Well, Nathan." Scott smiled, refusing to be provoked. "It's not my decision. Wolf Man decides whether you meet the wolves or not."

What Scott said only seemed to make Nathan more surly. "Wolf Man?" he demanded. "Who's this stupid Wolf Man? Why's he such a big deal? I thought *you* were the boss around here."

"I am," said Scott. "But Wolf Man looks after the wolves. He even lives in there with them. And *he* says who goes into the enclosure."

"Well, Wolf Man can get lost," said Nathan.

"He's not telling me what to do. And I want my mobile back. You got no right to confiscate our mobiles!"

"It's camp policy," explained Scott, patiently. "You've been told that already. No mobiles. You're here to learn the way of the wolf. And wolves don't need mobiles."

Nathan glowered. His eyes, hot and restless, flickered around. "Where's this wolf guy anyhow?"

Scott checked his watch. "He'll be along soon," he said.

Ellis felt as impatient as Nathan. He was curious about the mysterious Wolf Man. He hadn't had the chance to meet him yet.

"I know, kids!" Scott was telling the Wolf Campers. "While we're waiting for Wolf Man, let's see some wilderness skills!"

The red-haired boy butted in. "But we ain't in the wilderness."

He's right, thought Ellis. They were only three metro stops from the city. Wolf Camp was an artificial wilderness, specially created on an old industrial site. The first two wolves had been raised here from cubs. Scott had told Ellis how Wolf Man had cared for them, licking their fur, chewing up their meat into baby mush, just like a mother wolf would have done.

Scott ignored the red-haired boy's interruption. "Ellis here will give you a demonstration. He's the best there is at tracking animals or people. He's a tracking genius! I guarantee you'll be impressed!"

Ellis cringed again. Scott was a nice guy. But, sometimes, like Nathan, Ellis wished he would just shut up.

As Ellis expected, Scott's over-the-top praise had made him a target. Slowly, Nathan's scowling face swung towards him. He didn't seem impressed at all.

"What, him back there?" Nathan sneered. "A genius? You must be joking."

Ellis raised his steady grey eyes towards Nathan. Nathan was used to kids being scared of him. But he couldn't see any fear in Ellis's eyes. He tried to stare Ellis down. But Ellis didn't flinch. It was Nathan who had to look away first.

"This *demonstration* had better be good," muttered Nathan, menacingly.

Scott Spenser was busy explaining: "Okay, kids,"

he said, eagerly. "Here's the set-up. You're pirates, right?"

Nathan rolled his eyes, as if to say, *Pirates? Give me a break!*

"And you're going to bury this treasure," Scott continued. He took a slim gold bar out of his pocket. He handed it to one of the boys to look at. "Careful, it's heavy."

"Wow, is it real gold?" someone asked.

"Think they'd trust us with a real gold bar?" jeered Nathan. "Bad boys like us? We'd just nick it, wouldn't we?"

More boys laughed, big loud guffaws this time.

"Anyhow," said Scott, rushing on, as if he sensed he was losing control. "Me and Ellis will stay here, in the cabin. You all go down past the pond. Beyond it is a muddy field. When you get there, one of you buries the treasure in the field."

"I'll bury it," said Nathan, snatching the gold bar. "Anything to get this stupid pirate thing over with."

"Well, okay," Scott agreed. "So Nathan will bury it. And Ellis will follow his footprints right to the gold. But to make it difficult, the rest of you stomp around in the field. Cover up Nathan's tracks, try any trick you can. And Ellis will still find the treasure. Can you do that?" Scott asked Ellis.

Ellis shrugged. "Sure."

"It's just a bit of fun," added Scott.

Ellis made no comment. Although, privately, he agreed with Nathan. This wasn't proper tracking. It was more like a little kids' party game.

"It's a con," sneered Nathan. "Bet he peeks out the window, watches me bury it."

"You can't even see the field from here!" Scott protested.

Then, for the first time Ellis spoke directly to Nathan, as if there were only the two of them in the room. "Take me outside with you," he said. "Then blindfold me. Watch me all the time. Make sure I don't peek."

"We'll blindfold you now," said Nathan, springing up.

He snatched a black bandana from another boy's head and tied it, savagely tight, round Ellis's eyes. He gripped Ellis's arms, wrenched them behind his back, deliberately digging in strong fingers, with ragged, chewed nails. As he pushed Ellis, stumbling, towards the door, Ellis could hear Scott spluttering in the background, "Hey, no need to be so rough."

Ellis felt himself being dragged over rough, grassy ground.

"Stay here," said Nathan, finally releasing him. "Don't look round. I'll be watching."

Ellis couldn't *see* a thing. But his other senses were on red alert. He could smell mud and scummy pond water, feel the cool breeze, hear wind rustling the leaves. He could hear the boys' shrill, excited voices somewhere behind him.

He heard someone coming. "You okay, Ellis?" called Scott Spenser, anxiously. "Nathan was too rough back there. That was totally out of order. I should stop this right now."

"No!" said Ellis. He was scared Scott's interfering might make things worse. And besides, this wasn't Scott's business any more. He'd set up this stupid demonstration. But it was personal now, between Ellis and Nathan.

"Don't come any nearer," Ellis told Scott. "They'll think you're giving me clues."

"Okay," said Scott doubtfully. "If you're sure." Ellis heard his footsteps padding off over the grass.

Ellis waited, in the dark.

Scott's words, *It's just a bit of fun*, echoed in his head. Ellis smiled grimly. What was supposed to be fun was fast becoming something very sinister.

Ellis felt hot breath on his neck. Felt his head jerked back as Nathan untied the blindfold. Ellis blinked and staggered. Little sparkling lights danced before his eyes. Then everything clicked back into focus.

"Come on, tracking genius," sneered Nathan, gripping his arm again. "Find the buried treasure."

The boys were standing outside the field gate. Some had wide, mocking grins on their faces as if they'd already outwitted him. Ellis's mind tried to grapple with that. What had they been up to, all that time he'd been waiting? What sneaky tricks had they tried to confuse him?

They're probably clever tricks, Ellis warned himself, *if Nathan thought of them.*

Ellis didn't underestimate Nathan. He was a dangerous enemy. He was smart and manipulative. He could run rings round Scott, that was for sure.

Where is *Scott?* Ellis wondered briefly. Then Ellis saw him, hovering in the background. But it was Nathan, not Scott, who was in charge now.

Nathan tried to hustle Ellis through the gate. But Ellis was sick of being pushed around. He shook free of Nathan's grip and said, "I go in alone." Surprisingly, Nathan fell back. "I'm watching you, tracker boy," he warned.

Ellis heard a snigger from one of the Wolf Campers. "Bet you don't find the gold bar."

"Shut up!" ordered Nathan.

But Ellis was even surer now that they'd done something extra sneaky.

He walked alone into the middle of the wide, muddy field. His shoulders ached with tension. He could feel eyes boring into his back, watching his every move.

The field was a trampled mess of footprints. Some were blurred, almost wiped out by others. Tracks criss-crossed, went in circles, doubled back on themselves. It looked like a hopeless jumble.

Ellis squatted down to study them. He became focused, like he always did when tracking. The world outside, the people watching, ceased to exist.

He could pick out, immediately, which tracks belonged to which Wolf Camper. That's why he'd checked their shoes earlier, just in case. And footprints told him a lot about the person that made them: how they moved, even their mood.

These were the twitchy, red-haired kid's trainers. He'd been going crazy – running, jumping, even skidding along on his knees.

The boy that made these prints was heavy, left-handed, hesitant. That was the shy, dark-haired boy, whose bandana Nathan had snatched.

And here were Nathan's, the ones Ellis had been looking for. If he could trace them, through the chaos of other prints, they'd lead him straight to the buried treasure. He almost lost them in a scuffle of prints. Then he saw them leading away. But there was something odd about them now. They were Nathan's boots, but it wasn't Nathan wearing them. The prints weren't deep enough for his weight and height. And this person walked totally differently to Nathan's confident, swaggering gait.

A slow smile spread over Ellis's face. *Clever*, he thought. Nathan had set a false trail. He had swapped shoes with bandana boy.

Ellis knew now why the Wolf Campers had been smirking at the gate.

Ellis doubled back, found bandana boy's trainer

prints. That was Nathan wearing his shoes, no mistake. Ellis felt he was close to the treasure now. And here was a patch of freshly dug soil.

This is the place, thought Ellis, immediately.

He almost started digging.

But a sixth sense, that intuition that all good trackers have, stopped him.

This was all too easy. If Nathan had taken so much trouble with the shoe-swapping trick, why hadn't he disguised where he'd buried the treasure better – patted the soil smooth, or stomped on top of it?

Ellis studied Nathan's prints leading away from the freshly dug soil. He smiled again. It was a double bluff. Nathan hadn't buried the gold at all. He'd only pretended to. In fact, he still had it with him. Probably in his left jacket pocket. Ellis knew that because carrying the heavy bar made Nathan, very slightly, drag his left leg.

A mocking shout came from the gate.

"Do you give up yet, tracker boy?"

Ellis scrambled up from his knees. He didn't like Nathan. He thought he was a creep. But you had to admit he was cunning and quick-thinking.

I could have been digging in this field all day, thought Ellis, *and never found that bar*. Because it wasn't there.

But Ellis was certain now where it was. It was time to confront Nathan.

Ellis strolled, empty-handed, back to the gate. He saw that, just like he'd expected, Nathan was wearing his own boots again.

As Ellis reached them, the Wolf Campers found it hard not to show their glee. They thought Ellis had given up. Only Nathan's glare made them freeze their faces, draw back, as Ellis and Nathan stood facing each other.

Ellis was tired of being taken for a fool. He came straight to the point.

"You didn't bury the bar. You've got it in your left-hand jacket pocket."

Nathan tried hard not to look surprised. But he couldn't help it. The shock showed in his face. He didn't like to be beaten. He hadn't, for one second, expected it. He felt humiliated. And that made him *really* mad.

Even worse, there were admiring murmurs from some of the younger boys.

"Ellis knew exactly where it was!"

"How'd he know that? It's magic!"

Ellis shrugged. "Look, it's not magic or anything. Tracking's just what I do. It's no big deal."

But to Nathan, it was a very big deal. His face was stormy, twisting with uncontrollable rage. Then he completely lost it. He screamed insults at Ellis, spit flying from his mouth. Then something glinted in his right hand. Nathan had grabbed the gold bar from inside his jacket.

He suddenly lashed out, swinging it like a weapon. If it had connected, the metal bar could have cracked Ellis's skull. But Ellis had already sprung back.

Scott came shoving through the crowd of excited boys. "Hey, no violence allowed at Wolf Camp," he was shouting. "It's *absolutely* forbidden!"

Scott had guts, beneath that mild manner. He yelled at the other Wolf Campers: "Go back to the cabins! Move!" Then he tried to calm Nathan down.

"Let's stop this now," he told Nathan, his palms patting the air, in a peace-making gesture. "This has all gone way too far."

But Ellis knew Nathan was beyond calming. His

eyes were crazy, like a mad dog's. He was slashing around wildly with the metal bar, so no one could get close.

"Don't come near me!" he screamed.

Scott moved clumsily forward. Ellis thought, *He's going to get hurt!* So Ellis lowered his head and charged. He headbutted Nathan in the stomach. Nathan staggered back, winded. He almost fell. But somehow, he stayed on his feet. And he still held the metal bar.

What now? thought Ellis, trying to work out his next move.

But then behind Nathan, Ellis saw a lean figure slide out from the trees. It dropped into a crouching run and seemed to glide, with incredible speed, through the long grass. Now Scott saw it too.

"Wolf Man," he murmured.

Wolf Man crept from the bushes. Nathan still wasn't aware of him. Until Wolf Man whispered softly, right in his ear, "Drop the weapon."

And Nathan was so startled that he did.

It was all over in seconds. Wolf Man picked up the bar and sent it flying through the air in a golden arc. It splashed into the pond and sank.

Ellis felt his stomach unknot, the tension wash from his body, leaving him limp and shaking.

Nathan stood panting, bewildered, all the fight gone out of him. He seemed relieved too, that he'd been disarmed. As if he'd been scared of his own craziness, of what he might do next.

Now there was nothing left to see, the Wolf Campers, who'd been watching from a distance, turned and trailed back to the cabin.

Scott told Nathan, "I should throw you out of Wolf Camp right this minute!"

But he didn't actually do anything. He seemed to be waiting for Wolf Man to decide.

But Wolf Man stayed silent. His pale grey eyes were fixed on the far horizon, as if he was seeing things they couldn't. As if he was thinking about something much more important than this tiny incident.

Ellis took a closer look at him. Wolf Man wore a T-shirt and faded jeans. Ellis was surprised to see how old he was. He could be eighty, even older, it was hard to tell. Long silvery-white hair flowed down his back. His face was tanned and lined, with a hooked nose and high cheekbones, like an Apache chief. Ellis had just seen him move like a streak of lightning. But now there was a quiet stillness about him, a dignity that made even Nathan hesitate.

Then, at last, Wolf Man spoke. "So you want to meet the wolves?"

"You talking to me?" asked Nathan, some of the old swagger coming back into his voice.

Wolf Man, still gazing into the distance, answered with a silent nod. "So you want to meet the wolves?" he asked again in that same serene voice.

"I'm not bothered," said Nathan.

"Follow me then," said Wolf Man.

Ellis stood amazed as Wolf Man walked off with light springy steps, straight as a spear, towards the wolf enclosure, while Nathan stumbled after him.

For a moment, Scott stood speechless. But then he seemed to get really angry. "That Wolf Man!" he spat out. "He's on a different planet!"

Ellis stared at him, shocked. There was a rage in Scott's voice that he'd never heard before.

"He just *totally* ignores Wolf Camp rules," said Scott, bitterly. "I tell the new arrivals, 'You have to *earn* the right to meet the wolves. It's a *privilege* for good behaviour!' Then what does Wolf Man do?

He takes a vicious little thug like Nathan in there. After he tries to attack someone!"

Ellis shuffled about uncomfortably. He didn't know what to say. He'd had no idea Scott resented Wolf Man so much. But Scott raved on, as if he was talking to himself.

"I mean, I've got my own key to the enclosure," Scott was fuming. "But I don't go in often. Wolf Man doesn't like it. He makes that quite clear. But *I'm* a wolf expert too. *I've* been round the world, recording myths and folk tales about them. I know every wolf legend there is!"

Ellis glanced at his watch. "Look, can I go now?" he asked Scott.

Scott broke off his furious outburst. He looked down, startled, as if he'd forgotten Ellis was even there. "What?" he said.

"Can I go now?" Ellis repeated. "Only a boy is coming to the Natural History Museum. At least his body is. They call him Tattooed Boy. He's prehistoric. Some climbers found him in a glacier and dug him out."

"Tattooed Boy?" Scott asked Ellis, with sudden interest. "What kind of tattoos has he got?"

"Er, swirling blue ones, I think," said Ellis, surprised by Scott's question. "Covering his whole body, according to the Prof. Anyway, I've got to go," Ellis insisted. "Scott? Scott?"

But Scott was standing in a dream. Once again, his mind was far away. His eyes seemed dark and troubled. Then, suddenly, he shook himself, as if to focus on the present.

"Look, sorry about today," he told Ellis. "Things got a bit out of hand."

Ellis shrugged. "No one got hurt," he said. "So are you going to chuck Nathan out of Wolf Camp?"

"I should do," said Scott. Then he added, after a pause, "But I hate giving up on any kid. So we'll see."

Ellis hurried towards the metro station. As he went out of Wolf Camp, he wondered where Meriel was.

But he knew she'd turn up when she wanted to. And he wasn't worried about her. Meriel could look after herself.

CHAPTER THREE

Meriel was doing her favourite thing – flying. She gave a harsh croak, *"Krawk!"* and hung on the wind, her beady eyes searching the woods below for any signs of the wolf pack.

Her feathers were deep black. But when the sun hit her back they became iridescent, glossed with purple, green and blue.

"Krawk!" she called again.

She moved on with a strong wingbeat, then glided, searching the ground. She drifted, kept steady...

"Oh no!" Meriel scowled.

Suddenly she couldn't feel the wind ruffling her feathers, or the sun on her back.

Without any warning, she'd been grounded, whisked back to her own human body.

Meriel cursed her luck. It felt cruel, being snatched from the skies like that. But her power to mind-read animals had always been unpredictable. Sometimes it worked, sometimes it didn't. Sometimes, she could share a wild creature's mind for ages. Sometimes, like today, it ended in seconds.

Now she was earth-bound again, a small, skinny, tangle-haired girl, crouching behind a bush in the wolf enclosure.

She glanced upward. The raven she'd just been mind-reading was still soaring above her. Its body, big as a buzzard's, made a cross shape against the sky.

Prof. Talltrees had told her that, in the past, humans had feared ravens. They were birds of ill omen. Their croaking call foretold death. They gathered in sinister flocks before battles, waiting to peck out the eyes of fallen warriors.

Meriel had grinned when the Prof told her that. She loved mind-reading creatures that humans dreaded. Like ravens. Or wolves.

The raven swooped away over the trees, then folded its wings and dived like a thunderbolt. Meriel couldn't see where it landed.

I bet it's found the wolves, she thought.

Ravens and wolves are like best mates. They hang around together. They help each other out. Ravens can spy dead animals from the sky. But they can't rip them up, or crunch bones, like wolves can. So they fly down and guide the wolf pack to their dinner, hopping along in front. And, in return, the wolves let the ravens have the leftovers.

Meriel sighed. If only she'd been able to stay in the raven's mind a few minutes longer, she would have found the wolves too.

"Think...think," she told herself, trying to recall something she'd seen from the sky, through the raven's eyes. Any clues that might help her guess the wolves' location.

But it was unpredictable too, what she remembered from mind-reading wild creatures. Sometimes every detail was clear and vivid. Sometimes she only had flashbacks. And sometimes she remembered nothing at all.

Today her memory was sketchy.

"Think! Think!" she ordered herself again, her face screwed up in concentration.

But thinking was definitely *not* one of Meriel's favourite things. It made her head ache too much. It was what humans did. And Meriel always tried to deny she was human, with a human heart and brain. She identified most with the creatures she mind-read. It was their world she longed to be part of.

Meriel wouldn't care if all humans were wiped off the face of the earth. Except Ellis, of course, and Professor Talltrees. And a few other people she'd met on missions. She'd be sad if anything happened to them.

Meriel clenched her fists in angry frustration. She wasn't a patient person like Ellis. She couldn't bear waiting. She wanted results straight away.

"Stop thinking!" she ordered herself. "Thinking will drive you crazy."

Thinking was the main reason Meriel couldn't mind-read people. It made their minds so busy, such a tangled mess. Animal minds were simple by comparison.

Then Meriel gasped out loud. Now she'd stopped thinking, her mind was clear, receptive. A sudden picture flashed into it, of something she'd just seen from the sky. A mass of blurry red, rippling like the sea, blazing like fire. A big circle of white light, with dark shapes prowling in it. Almost immediately, it faded.

But Meriel smiled. Her fierce eyes glittered with excitement. She had all the clues she needed.

She shinned up the nearest tree, to get a bird's-eye view over the wild wolf enclosure. She was, roughly, at the centre of the wood. A forest of trees spread out in each direction.

"There!" she whispered to herself.

To the west was that sea of fiery red. It was a grove of maple trees with scarlet leaves, enclosing that circle of bright light – a sun-filled clearing.

Meriel wasn't high enough to see inside the clearing. But she gave a grunt of satisfaction. She knew what was in there all right, what those dark prowling shapes were that the raven had dived towards.

"Wolves," she told herself, with a big, happy grin.

She climbed down the tree and headed for the grove of scarlet maples.

She shouldn't have been inside the wolf enclosure at all. When she'd reached the main gate, huge warning signs had said, *Danger! Strictly NO Entry!* Those signs meant nothing to Meriel. She lived by her own laws, not human ones.

The main gate had been locked. It had wicked spikes at the top and razor wire. So did the high fence all around the enclosure.

I can't climb in, Meriel had thought, dismayed.

It was Travis, her weasel, who'd found another way, a weak place at the bottom of the fence where the wire had ripped. He'd flowed through easily, like a red, furry snake. But Meriel had had to bend back the wire to make the opening larger. And even then she'd snagged her clothes. After she'd got through, she'd bent the wire carefully back into place.

"Wolves escaping into the city," Meriel had told

herself, shaking her head. "Not a good idea."

It wasn't the people she was worried about – but the wolf pack. People mostly hated wolves. They'd go hysterical. The wolves would be shot by police marksmen.

Now Meriel hurried on, towards those scarlet trees. That's where the Wolf Camp pack was. She was sure of it.

"Be careful, Travis," she murmured, as she ran.

Once through the fence, the weasel had gone bounding off, his sharklike eyes glittering, searching for prey.

Travis was a fearsome hunter and recklessly brave. He'd fight to the death if cornered. But there were big dangers for him in the wolf enclosure. First, from the wolves themselves. They were fed a dead deer every day – Meriel had just passed the gnawed and bloody bones of their most recent meal – but they'd hunt small mammals for themselves: squirrels, rabbits, weasels.

Then there were ravens, with their brutal stabbing beaks. They wouldn't say no to a weasel snack. A picture flashed into her mind – of Travis dead, with his eyes pecked out.

Scowling, Meriel tossed her head as if to shake out the picture, making her wild, tangled hair fly about.

"Go away!" she ordered it.

That was her human side, tormenting her with nightmares, making her fret about things that might never happen. That human heart, Meriel often thought, was a big inconvenience.

Her animal side knew that life was risky. Nature was red in tooth and claw and Travis would just have to take his chances. That was how it was. No amount of worrying would change it.

Meriel had reached the maple grove now. Scarlet leaves trembled above her head.

She dropped to the ground and crawled, commando-style, to the clearing. She wasn't scared of the wolves. She just didn't want them to run away. She wanted to watch them and, most of all, to mind-read them. She wanted to know what it felt like, being a wolf.

And there they were, right in front of her, four adult wolves and two cubs. They were sprawled out, dozing in the sun. Her raven, the one she'd mind-read, hopped about amongst them. The wolves could have killed it with one snap. But wolves never ever hurt ravens. They need them too much.

Meriel gave a long, drawn-out sigh of contentment. She snuggled down into the long grass. She was downwind of the wolves, so they couldn't smell her. And if she stayed very quiet, they'd never know she was there.

She sniffed at the grass. There was a strong, musky wolf smell all around, where they'd been peeing. That meant, *Keep off! This is our territory!*

Then suddenly, the raven croaked an alarm call. It took off in a clatter of wings. What had it seen? Meriel forgot about mind-reading. She lifted her nose like a dog and sniffed the air. She smelled people!

Then she saw them, coming through the trees on the far side of the clearing, a man with long, flowing hair and a slouching boy. Meriel snarled softly.

"Go away!" she whispered, furiously. People spoiled everything.

But the people kept on coming. Then they stopped in the trees on the edge of the clearing. They seemed to be talking.

Meriel bared her teeth at them again. Then, as

shy and wary of people as any wolf, she wriggled backwards, sprang to her feet and vanished like a ghost into the trees. But she didn't go far. Instead, she began circling round to get behind them. She wanted to listen.

Wolf Man shaded his eyes. "Thought I saw something," he said to Nathan. "Over there, in the trees."

But there was nothing there now. He shook his head and, still concealed in the trees, he pointed out each member of the wolf pack to Nathan.

"That black one's Storm, the pack leader," said Wolf Man, keeping his voice low. "And that's Star – see the white star mark on her forehead? She's his mate. Then there's Grey and Dancer, their two cubs from last year. They're grown up now. And this year's cubs are only ten weeks old. They haven't got names yet."

Storm got up and stretched lazily. He was a big, majestic wolf, black with a white throat and belly, and golden eyes.

He patted a cub out of the way with his paw. The tiny kitten-like fur ball rolled and squealed. But Storm hadn't hurt it. He'd been deliberately gentle, held back his power. It was just to remind the cub who was boss.

"I want to meet *him*," said Nathan, pointing. "That big wolf."

"Not yet," said Wolf Man.

"I said I want to," insisted Nathan.

Wolf Man's voice had been courteous so far. But now it took on an edge of steel.

"This isn't about what *you* want," he said to Nathan.

Nathan looked confused and angry: "I came here to meet the wolves, didn't I? You said I could. And now you're messing me about!"

Neither of them saw Meriel, hidden in the bracken, close enough to watch them, hear what they were saying.

Wolf Man's grey eyes grew stern. "Look, let's get something straight," he said to Nathan. "I don't care what you were before. Whether you were a gang leader, top dog in your neighbourhood. I don't care about your past, your family background. That means nothing here. You're in the wolves' world now. You live by their rules."

"Their rules?" protested Nathan. "I thought you

were the big boss! They call you Wolf Man, don't they? I thought you trained them or something!"

For the first time, Wolf Man's grave, hawkish face broke into a grin. "What, like pet dogs? To do tricks, fetch sticks and beg? You must be joking," he said. "I've got nothing to teach a wolf. If I'm lucky, they might teach me a thing or two."

In the bracken, Meriel looked surprised. She was seldom interested in humans. But this one, it seemed, knew at least a little bit about wolves.

"There's a little hideout here," Wolf Man told Nathan.

Where? thought Meriel.

Then she saw it, a little hut, beautifully made of woven branches, that blended into the trees. Wolf Man had built it himself. It was so well camouflaged that, if Wolf Man hadn't showed it to Nathan, Meriel might have missed it.

"You can watch what I do from in there," said Wolf Man. "But stay put. Whatever you do, don't show yourself. The wolves aren't used to you yet."

Then, leaving Nathan watching from the hut, Wolf Man walked, very slowly, out from the trees, into the clearing.

Hidden in the trees, Meriel was watching too. Despite herself, she was curious. She wanted to see how this human behaved. Wolves always avoid humans if they can. But this guy was taking a big risk. He was deliberately provoking them, on their own territory, walking right into the middle of their pack.

He'd better *know a bit about wolves*, thought Meriel. If he made the wrong move, the pack might turn on him. And it would be his own fault.

Serves him right, thought Meriel. *You don't mess around with wolves.*

Wolf Man walked into the centre of the sunny clearing. Storm stalked up to investigate, with his mate Star. Even though she'd known Wolf Man for years, Star snarled, bared her teeth. She had cubs to protect, she couldn't afford to take chances.

Immediately, Wolf Man crouched low, made himself small to show he wasn't a challenge. Storm sniffed him, then licked his face to show he was welcome to the pack. Wolf Man had raised Star and Storm from cubs. But every time he approached the pack he had to go through this ritual to make sure the wolves accepted him.

In the trees, Meriel was surprised for a second time. This guy knew *a lot* about wolves. He knew how to behave around them.

He's doing all right, she thought, nodding in grudging approval. He didn't try to take control, the way humans usually did. He was being respectful to Storm, the wolves' chosen leader.

Then the mood changed, completely. Because Nathan came out of the hut. He swaggered out into the clearing, walking tall, defiant, as if he owned the place. Making himself the centre of attention. Immediately, the wolves reacted. Star saw the stranger and growled. Grey and Dancer loped up to protect her.

Meriel sucked her breath in through her teeth. *There's going to be trouble*, she thought.

But Wolf Man didn't seem too concerned. He'd taken boys like Nathan into the wolf enclosure before. They almost never did what they were told. They often deliberately did the opposite. Until they learned their lesson.

"Go back, Nathan," Wolf Man told him, in a calm, controlled voice. "Walk back, slowly, to the hut."

But, just like he'd expected, Nathan didn't turn round.

And it was too late anyway. Storm's golden eyes were fixed on Nathan, in an unblinking wolf stare.

In the trees, Meriel felt a tingle of excitement down her spine. It looked like things were turning nasty. She knew that wolf stare. She used it herself sometimes. It meant Storm felt threatened. It meant he thought Nathan wanted to take over his pack.

Now all four wolves were in a line, facing Nathan. Nathan stopped, confused. For the first time, fear showed in his face. As if he was thinking, too late, *Why didn't I listen to Wolf Man?*

Storm's fur was bristling. He arched his back. A low menacing growl rumbled up from his belly. He pulled his lips back, baring sharp white fangs.

"Get down," Wolf Man ordered Nathan. "Onto the ground."

But Nathan stood frozen, too scared to move. Then Storm crouched. That crouch meant, *Watch out! I'm going to attack!*

Wolf Man had his next move clear in his mind. He planned to crawl towards Nathan, drag him down. Make Storm see the boy wasn't a challenge.

And make Nathan see that this was a world where wolves ruled. Wolf Man had already told Nathan that. But he knew Nathan wouldn't believe it. Not until he'd found out for himself, the hard way.

Suddenly, a figure came darting out from the bracken. And all Wolf Man's plans were shot to pieces.

It's a girl! thought Wolf Man. *What's she doing here?*

His eyes flickered round. How would the wolves react? It didn't look good. Grey was growling, getting himself all worked up. He was much more jumpy than Storm, a young hothead. He could explode into violence any second.

Wolf Man's mind raced, juggling options.

Deal with Grey first, he decided. Wolf Man didn't have time for respectful rituals. He stared straight into Grey's eyes. Forcing him to back down, like an alpha wolf would.

While Wolf Man and Grey locked eyes, Meriel dived for Nathan's knees. He crumpled; Meriel rolled out the way.

She slithered back over to Nathan as he sprawled on the ground. She ripped down his jacket zip.

"Hey!" said Nathan.

Now a triangle of white T-shirt showed at his neck.

Wolf Man risked a quick sideways glance and saw what she'd done. *This girl knows about wolves*, he thought, amazed.

What she did next convinced him even more.

"Whimper," Meriel ordered Nathan. She made whimpering noises like a pup, to show him what to do.

But Nathan's brain was still scrambled by fear. He tried to get up. "No," said Meriel. "Stay down, stupid!"

But Nathan's struggling had upset Storm. He was starting his run, growling, his mouth wide open to show white fangs, red throat.

"Now look what you've done!" Meriel accused Nathan, angrily.

Then, suddenly, a fat little fur ball, one of the pups, came bouncing over. Storm braked immediately, his big front paws raking the ground. He crouched, watching.

"Hiya," Meriel greeted the cub. "Where were you hiding?"

The pup climbed on Nathan's body, its stubby tail wagging. It licked Nathan's face, giving shrill yips of excitement. It wanted to play.

But Nathan still thought he was under attack.

"Gerroff!" he cried, trying to push it off.

"No!" said Meriel. She showed him what to do. "Play!" she said to Nathan. "Play!"

Nathan stared at her, this strange girl with the fierce gaze, who'd appeared from nowhere and rugby-tackled him to the ground. "Play?" he repeated, bewildered, as if he didn't understand the word.

"You heard her," hissed Wolf Man, without turning his head. "Just do what she says."

He couldn't move to help. He was still in a stare-out with Grey. Grey had moved closer, so man and wolf were face-to-face. Wolf Man could smell Grey's hot meaty breath, see his own twin reflection in Grey's golden eyes.

But, somehow, Wolf Man wasn't afraid for Nathan. It seemed like the girl could handle the situation. She was a natural with wolves. Wolf Man had never seen anything like it.

Storm stood by, still giving low snarls. Star left Dancer and stalked over to join him, watching suspiciously. Meriel nuzzled the pup's face. It licked her back, then it growled, pretending to be a grown-up wolf. Cautiously, Meriel rose to all fours. Storm snarled again but didn't stop her. The pup pounced at her. It wanted a play fight. Meriel knew she'd have to be careful. If Star thought her cub was in any danger, she'd instantly defend it.

"*Grrr,*" said Meriel, softly headbutting the pup.

It tumbled over, with squeals of joy.

The other one came waddling over, a bloody scrap of rabbit skin in its jaws. It thrust the stinking fur again and again in Nathan's face.

"*Yurgh!*" Nathan protested.

"Calm down," said Meriel, in her cool, scornful voice. "It only wants to play tug of war."

At last, Nathan seemed to grasp that Meriel was on his side, trying to help him. He pushed himself onto all fours, grabbed the fur.

"Be gentle," warned Meriel, whose wolf puppy playmate was nipping her ear. Storm and Star were still standing guard, their alert eyes following every move.

The tiny wolf cub began the game, trying to tug and growl at the same time. Nathan had the sense to let it win. After a few shakes, he let go of the fur, as if the pup was too strong for him.

The wolf cub raced off with its trophy, its stubby tail wagging furiously. Then it came hurtling back and flung itself at Nathan.

"*Ow, ow*," said Nathan, falling over, pretending the tiny bundle of fur had knocked him down.

At last, Star and Storm loped away, satisfied their cubs were in no danger. Grey saw his parents go. He lost interest in Wolf Man and wandered after them. All four adult wolves flopped on the grass, panting, their pink tongues lolling out. They looked totally relaxed. They seemed to have accepted Nathan, for the moment. And it was mostly down to that girl.

Who is she? Wolf Man wondered. She knew a great deal about wolves.

She knew, for instance, to show Nathan's T-shirt. Sometimes a flash of white at your throat will calm an angry wolf. That's because, among wolves, it's a sign of surrender when you roll over and show your white throat fur.

Now she was warning Nathan again, "Stay down!" It wasn't time yet to get to his feet. Storm might still think it was a challenge.

But Nathan was too busy, playing in the dirt like a little kid. Both cubs were swarming all over him, giving him sharp puppy nips, practising for killing deer when they were older.

"*Ow*, that hurts," said Nathan.

But he didn't lash out. He kept back his power like he'd seen Storm do.

With his wise grey eyes, Wolf Man noticed that. Was Nathan already learning from wolves? It was far too soon to be sure. But something had told him that it was worth taking a chance on Nathan. Where Scott saw a violent, swaggering thug, Wolf Man had seen a kind of despair in Nathan's eyes that said, *Help me!*

You could still be wrong about him, Wolf Man warned himself. This was only Nathan's first contact with wolves. If he felt superior to them, or was too arrogant, then he wouldn't learn anything.

"*Grrr*," Nathan said gently to the puppies, who dashed off in delight, pretending he was a fierce creature.

Nathan even seemed to be having fun. Wolf Man wondered how long it had been since tough boy Nathan had played and had fun.

Wolf Man crawled over to Meriel, keeping his body low. He didn't want to risk upsetting Storm again.

"Who *are* you?" he whispered to her. "What's your name?"

Meriel didn't seem to have heard the question. A wolf cub pounced on her trainer, pretending it was a rabbit. Now it tried to bite it to death with its sharp puppy teeth.

"*Ooo*, you're scary," Meriel told the tiny cub, not minding if her trainer was chewed to shreds.

"You know a lot about wolves," Wolf Man persisted.

At last, Meriel turned to look at him. He was shocked to see that her eyes weren't quite human. They had a savage, cold glitter that reminded him of a bird of prey.

"You know a lot about wolves," he repeated.

"*Huh!*" said Meriel, dismissing that with a haughty toss of her head. "Actually, I *don't* know a lot about wolves. This is the first time I've met any." Then she added. "But wolves and wild dogs do some things the same. And I was raised by wild dogs. At least until I was two."

Wolf Man stared at her. "What?" He'd seen a lot of things in his life and not much surprised him. But he was surprised now, and fascinated.

"You're not going, are you?" he asked her, as she scrambled up, carefully shaking the wolf cub from her shoe. He wanted to ask her more about her past. Had she really said she'd been raised by wild dogs? He'd completely forgotten that she shouldn't have been in here anyway. Not without his permission.

"Yes," said Meriel. "I'm going now."

For Meriel, this first meeting with wolves had been frustrating. She'd come here to mind-read one of them. But she couldn't do it, not now, with these humans cramping her style and ruining her concentration.

Never mind, she told herself. She'd come back to the wolf enclosure later, after midnight, when the humans were in bed and there was just her and the wolves.

But before she left, she wanted to say one thing. Ellis would have been gobsmacked if he'd heard her. Meriel never, ever apologized. And this sounded almost like an apology. Or would have, if Meriel hadn't said it so defiantly.

"I shouldn't have run out like that," she told Wolf Man, "and upset Grey."

"So why did you?" asked Wolf Man, curiously.

"Because I thought you couldn't handle things," said Meriel, in her usual brutally honest way. "But you could have. Probably."

She slipped across the clearing, with Wolf Man gazing after her. The wolf cub who'd tried to kill her shoe threw back its head. It let out a long, soulful puppy howl, as if it had lost its wolf sister.

Just before she reached the trees, Wolf Man yelled out, "You never told me your name!"

"Meriel," she shouted back over her shoulder. Then she vanished into the maple trees.

Meriel trotted back through the wood, heading for the place in the fence where she and Travis had got into the wolf enclosure. Every so often, she sucked at the skin on the back of her hand. The tiny shrill squeaks she made sounded just like an injured rat or rabbit. That would make Travis come running because he'd think he'd found easy prey.

And here he came, flowing up her body and draping himself round her neck.

"Come on, Travis," said Meriel. "We'll come

back later. When there are no people around."

After Meriel had gone, Wolf Man and Nathan stayed with the wolf pack. Wolf Man seemed completely at home.

But Nathan stared round warily, scared, now that weird girl wasn't here to guide him, of making a wrong move.

Wolf Man saw how twitchy he was. "Just chill out," he told Nathan. "Like the wolves."

Nathan thought, *Yeah, that's easy for you to say.*

But then a pup bounced over. It held a raven's feather it had found in its prickly teeth. It laid the feather, all chewed and draggled with mud, down in front of Nathan as if giving him something precious.

The pup backed away, then yelped – high-pitched puppy calls of distress. It had got itself tangled up in bramble. Nathan crawled over, tried to free it from the spiky loops.

Then his stomach tightened. Storm, the lordly pack leader, was loping over to investigate. Did Storm think he was harming the pup? But Storm just gave Nathan a thorough sniffing and stalked off, as if he trusted him.

That gave Nathan the biggest thrill.

It amazed Nathan that Storm could trust him, when he hardly trusted himself. But the big, powerful pack leader seemed to have seen something in Nathan that most people, apart from Wolf Man, had missed.

Gradually, as the afternoon shadows lengthened, Nathan let his mind relax. The rage that was always burning inside him began to cool down. And Nathan suddenly, unexpectedly, felt happier and more protected among this pack of wild wolves than he'd ever felt anywhere.

As the sun set, the adult wolves seemed to come alive. With the cubs, they formed into a tight semicircle.

"What's happening?" Nathan asked Wolf Man. "What do I do?"

"Watch me," whispered Wolf Man.

He crawled on his hands and knees to join the wolf group. Nathan did the same. He was next to Grey. Grey stared at him steadily with amber eyes. Then turned his head away.

The wolves seemed to be waiting for something.

Then Storm threw back his head and started a deep, thrilling howl that seemed to echo everywhere in the still wood. One by one, the other wolves followed, even the cubs with their shrill piercing yips, until the whole pack were howling in chorus.

Nathan felt the eerie calls tingle like electricity through his whole body. Even the earth under his hands vibrated. Then Wolf Man threw back his head and added his voice. This time Nathan didn't sneer, like he had done when Scott howled.

Instead, without thinking twice, he joined in. His howl was hesitant at first, but then it grew stronger, more confident. Until it seemed totally natural, to be here in this twilit wood, singing this wild, ancient song alongside the wolves.

Storm stopped howling. It was like a signal. The other wolves stopped too, then Wolf Man. Nathan found himself howling alone. He stopped, embarrassed.

"You did well," Wolf Man praised him. "You gave a true wolf howl."

To his surprise, Nathan felt a strange glow warm his heart. It was pride in himself, an emotion he'd almost forgotten.

"Why'd they do that?" he asked Wolf Man. "That howling thing?"

"It's to warn other wolves they're here," said Wolf Man. "It means, 'Keep off. This is our territory.'"

"But there aren't any other wolves," said Nathan.

"There are some, who've been released into the northern forests. And there's a captive pack in a safari park down south. They're hundreds of kilometres from here. But these wolves don't know that," said Wolf Man. "Besides, they like to howl. Look at them."

The wolves were dancing around each other, nuzzling and licking, as if howling had been a lot of fun.

"Come on," said Wolf Man. "Time to leave them alone. Time for you to go back to the cabins."

They began walking back, through the wolf enclosure, towards the main gate.

Nathan felt crushed by disappointment. "Have I got to go back? You mean to Scott and the others?"

"If Scott will have you," said Wolf Man.

Then Nathan remembered what he'd done, when he'd lost it and lashed out with that bar. All that had slipped his mind when he was with the wolf pack. He'd somehow hoped Wolf Man had forgotten too.

"Scott won't let me stay!" protested Nathan. "He'll chuck me out!"

"You can't blame him," said Wolf Man, suddenly stern. "But he's a good guy. He might be persuaded to change his mind. If you apologize."

Nathan frowned. "If I do," he said, "can I come and see the wolves tomorrow?"

"Yes," said Wolf Man. "You can do that."

Wolf Man let Nathan out of the main gate. "Aren't you coming too?" Nathan asked him.

"No," said Wolf Man, closing the gate and locking Nathan out. "I live in here."

Nathan bit his lip, as, from the other side of the fence, he watched Wolf Man turn around and walk back into the wood.

He could feel that old familiar rage rising again, burning like acid in his throat. He felt angry with the whole world, even Wolf Man.

I'm not going back to the cabins, decided Nathan, scowling.

It wasn't grovelling to Scott he minded. Scott didn't matter to him. It was being with the other

Wolf Campers. Having to be the old Nathan again, always being the hard man, acting tough and threatening. When he felt anything but tough inside.

He thought about being with the wolves. Where he'd been allowed, for the first time in years, to be something different.

He could still smell their musky scent on his clothes. *I'm going back to them*, Nathan suddenly decided.

And nothing was going to stop him.

He prowled round the perimeter fence of the wolf enclosure. He missed the place where Meriel had got in, under the wire, because she'd bent the wire back into place. But he found another way.

There was a huge, dying oak tree just outside the fence. Its trunk was tilting at a crazy angle, its roots ripped out of the ground. As it toppled, it had crashed into another tree, just *inside* the enclosure. The two trees' topmost branches had locked tightly together, making a sort of bridge over the fence.

Nathan stared upwards at the tree bridge.

I could crawl across that, thought Nathan. *Get back inside*.

He'd have to be careful though. It was only half a metre above the spikes that topped the fence. But the intertwined branches looked firm enough, as if they would take his weight.

Nathan scrambled, monkey-like, up the oak's sloping trunk. Then, lying on his belly, he slid out onto the tree bridge. It was only a short crossing, maybe four or five metres. And it was fine, until he reached the middle.

Whoa, thought Nathan. He was a city boy; he didn't realize tree branches could be this springy.

Suddenly, the centre of the bridge sagged, like a hammock. Now his belly was only centimetres from those wicked spikes and the coils of razor wire between them.

The bridge dropped again, just slightly, but with a sickening jolt.

"*Ow!*" Nathan felt a spike pricking his flesh. He sucked his stomach in.

He didn't dare move. He hardly dared breathe. He lay there, in a cold sweat.

He waited, trying to keep perfectly still.

"You're stuck here," Nathan told himself. He daren't go forward or back.

Suddenly, he started trembling. His whole body was shaking, he couldn't stop it. He felt the branches beneath him slump and sway, imagined those spikes in his guts, that razor wire slicing him open...

In a frenzy of panic he reached out, grabbed a leafy overhanging branch and hauled himself off the sagging bridge. He scrambled into the other tree and crouched there, hugging the trunk, feeling sick and dizzy. He glanced back, then wished he hadn't. He could see spikes poking up through the tree bridge, just where his belly had been. He'd almost been shish-kebabbed.

That made him start shaking all over again.

When he'd stopped, he swung down through the branches.

He leaped the last few metres, rolling on spongy cushions of moss.

I'm in! he thought, picking himself up.

He plunged into the trees, searching for the wolf pack.

It was dusk now. The trees were in shades of grey with deep dark shadows between them. But, suddenly, the moon slid out from behind a cloud.

As Nathan was running, it bathed the woods in a silver glow.

Wolf Man came out from behind a tree, where he'd been hiding.

Nathan had disobeyed him again. That didn't surprise Wolf Man one bit. But what did surprise him was that incredible tree-bridge crossing. What a crazy stunt! Wolf Man had held his breath watching. He'd almost rushed out to help. But before he could, Nathan had somehow clambered to safety.

"He's got spirit," Wolf Man murmured, shaking his head in admiration.

Perhaps his hunch about Nathan would pay off. Perhaps the boy would prove himself worthy to be with wolves.

CHAPTER FOUR

Ellis and Professor Talltrees were in a laboratory, down in the basement of the Natural History Museum. They were looking at an orange body bag on a steel trolley. Zipped inside the bag was the corpse of the Tattooed Boy, packed in ice.

Spread out on a lab bench by the trolley were the boy's possessions.

The Tattooed Boy had arrived like a VIP.

A helicopter had come swooping over the city. It had hovered over the Natural History Museum, then dropped, rotors *whop, whop, whopping*, onto the flat roof.

The body bag had been strapped to a stretcher on the outside of the copter. It seemed like a huge bag. Ellis thought, *That Tattooed Boy must have been a giant.*

It was heavy too. It took four men to carry the stretcher, then transfer the body bag to the waiting trolley.

Then it was rushed down in the lift to the laboratories in the museum basement.

"Can we just have one quick look at him?" Ellis asked the Prof.

The Prof frowned. "We should wheel him into a refrigeration chamber," he said, "before he thaws out too much."

But Ellis could see the Prof was tempted. It might be their last private moment alone with the Tattooed Boy. Tomorrow, several scientists would arrive, crowding around the corpse, trying to find out who he was, how he'd died.

The Prof rubbed at the scars on his face, thinking.

Along with the scars, he had other injuries. His left leg was lame; he walked with a limp. And he wore a black eyepatch to hide his empty left eye socket. The Prof had got these wounds eleven years ago when he'd rescued Meriel from her wild dog family.

He was a scary-looking figure, with his wrecked face. To many people he seemed a cold and forbidding boffin. Only Ellis and Meriel knew that, really, the Prof wasn't like that at all.

"Well, all right," the Prof finally decided. His scarred face broke into a sudden, boyish grin. "Just a quick look won't do any harm. And besides, who's to know?"

The Prof started unzipping the big body bag. Ellis felt slightly sick. But he was fascinated too, in a ghoulish kind of way.

The Prof brushed the crushed ice aside. There was another insulating layer underneath, some sort of shiny metal foil. Then more ice and more insulating stuff that the Prof carefully peeled away.

As he waited, Ellis's stomach was churning.

"Here he is," said the Prof, at last. "Want to come and see?"

Ellis stepped forward. He saw a shrivelled,

mummified body, small as a five-year-old child's inside all that packaging.

"How old was he?" said Ellis, gulping down his nausea. "He looks like a little kid. I thought he was a teenager,"

"He was," said the Prof. "About fourteen, fifteen, they think. But his body's shrunk after all that time in the ice."

The boy's limbs were twisted, bent at odd angles like a crushed spider. His skin was leathery brown, stretched tight, with bones poking through. The skull-like head was the size of a coconut, but bald, like a very old man's, with a few bristles of red hair. Some rags, all that remained of his tunic and trousers, still clung to his body.

"Look at his face!" said Ellis appalled.

It was a grisly sight. Two withered eyeballs were shrunk deep in the sockets. Broken teeth showed between mashed lips. And his nose was squashed, spread all over his face.

"Why is his face all battered like that?" asked Ellis.

But the Prof seemed to expect what he saw. "He's been under a glacier for five thousand years," said the Prof. "Moving ice exerts enormous forces. It can grind boulders to bits. I'm surprised he's so undamaged. Shame those clumsy climbers who dug him out didn't take more care. They used an ice axe – it broke right through his ribcage."

Ellis shuddered at the gaping black hole in the Tattooed Boy's chest.

"I can't see any tattoos," he said, coming closer.

The Prof said, "Here's one." He traced a faded black swirl on the Tattooed Boy's forehead. "They would have been blue originally," said the Prof. "And all over his face and body. And you can tell he once had red hair. He would have been tall too, for his age, before the ice crushed him."

Ellis stared at the mangled mess on the trolley. He tried to imagine the boy when he'd been alive. But he couldn't. His imagination just wouldn't make that leap.

"He would have been quite a striking figure," the Prof continued, "in his wolfskin cloak."

The Prof glanced over to the bench, where the Tattooed Boy's cloak lay spread out, along with his other possessions: his yew bow, his quiver of arrows, his copper axe, his dagger. And the belt with the leather pouch on it.

"Wolfskin?" said Ellis, surprised. "Where'd he get wolfskin from?"

These days, you usually only saw wolves in zoos, or at places like Wolf Camp if you were lucky.

"Wolves were common in this country then." The Prof shrugged. "There were some weird beliefs about them. That you could turn into one if you ate lycanthropous flowers—"

"*What* flowers?" interrupted Ellis.

"Lycanthropous," repeated the Prof. "*Lycanthrope* meaning werewolf. And warriors thought wearing cloaks made of wolfskin gave them a wolf's powers."

"So was the Tattooed Boy a warrior then?" asked Ellis. It was hard to believe, looking at the gruesome thing in the body bag that hardly even seemed human.

"I don't know," said the Prof. "But he had some fine weapons with him."

The Prof picked up the copper axe. "Apparently, he was found still clutching this. When they dug him up they prised it out of his hand. And they took off his wolfskin cloak."

They shouldn't have done that, thought Ellis.

He touched the cloak, fascinated. After five thousand years in the ice it had lost all its wolf fur. It looked like a tatty old scrap of leather.

Could it really have given the prehistoric boy wolf powers? Ellis glanced again at that pathetic, broken body.

"Cover him up," said Ellis, suddenly. It wasn't just because he felt squeamish. "It doesn't feel right to be gawping at him like this," he told the Prof.

The Prof nodded. He understood. Although he knew that, tomorrow, he and the other scientists would be doing worse things to the Tattooed Boy than just staring. They'd be studying every centimetre of him, giving him body scans, drilling into his skull, opening his stomach to examine its contents and find out what his last meal on earth had been, pawing through all his personal possessions.

"Hang on," said the Prof, as he was folding back the shiny metal sheet over the body. "What's that inside his chest?" he said, intrigued.

He pulled on a pair of thin, surgical gloves. Then he slid his fingers into the Tattooed Boy's gaping chest wound, and, very delicately, felt around.

"*Urgh!* What are you doing?" gasped Ellis. "I'm going to throw up!"

The Prof pulled out his hand. He was grasping something between his finger and thumb. "Look at that," he said, showing Ellis. "It's a flint arrowhead!"

Ellis was as amazed as his guardian. He forgot his sickness. "What's that doing in there?"

"Our Tattooed Boy was shot," said the Prof. "In the back, it looks like."

"Shot?" echoed Ellis. "Are you sure?"

"We'll know for certain tomorrow, when we start a full examination."

"So was he *murdered*?" asked Ellis.

The Prof said, "I don't know. Depends whether that arrow wound killed him. Or whether he froze to death."

"But you said he was shot in the *back*," said Ellis. "That means he was probably ambushed, or being chased, doesn't it?"

The Prof shook his head. "We can only guess. We'll probably never know the truth. Even after all the scientific tests."

The Prof felt the Tattooed Boy's skin. It was

getting spongy. "Better get him frozen up again," said the Prof.

"Wait a minute," said Ellis. "Look at his left wrist."

He hadn't noticed it before; round the Tattooed Boy's twiglike wrist was a thin, plaited band.

"*Hmmm*," said the Prof. "Looks like it's made from some kind of animal skin."

Ellis wore a plaited band on his left wrist too. It was so thin, most people didn't notice it. And anyhow, it was kept well hidden, under his sleeve. It was made out of python skin. It had been a gift from his parents, who were killed two years ago, by poachers, in Africa.

Ellis wondered if the Tattooed Boy's parents had given *him* his band, way back in prehistoric times.

The Prof said, "Those stupid climbers stripped him of everything else when they dug him up. They probably tried to take this off too. But it's sunk too deep in his flesh."

Working quickly, the Prof wrapped up the corpse, zipped up the body bag.

"I'll set the alarm," he said.

"What alarm?" asked Ellis.

"There's an alarm on the refrigeration chamber. It sounds through the building if the Tattooed Boy's temperature rises above a certain level."

"Why would his temperature rise?"

"If his refrigeration chamber breaks down. Or if it gets opened somehow."

"So what happens then?"

"His body starts to decompose, very quickly."

Ellis sniffed. Now the Prof mentioned it, with his keen tracker's sense of smell, he'd just caught a whiff of rotting flesh.

Then the Prof smelled it too.

"It's *definitely* time to put him in the deep freeze," he said.

The refrigeration chambers were in a small room attached to the lab, behind a blue door. The Prof wheeled the trolley through it.

Ellis relaxed a bit. He was glad that the Tattooed Boy's pitiful remains were hidden from view. It seemed more respectful somehow.

He picked up the Tattooed Boy's bow. *It's a beautiful bow*, he thought, admiring it. The Prof came back from the refrigeration room. "Think he made this bow himself?" Ellis asked his guardian.

"Probably," said the Prof. "It's amazing it's still in one piece."

The quiver of arrows looked crushed and battered. Some arrows inside were broken, but two were perfect, still fledged.

"If you put a string on that bow, you could still fire those arrows," said the Prof. "I'm guessing he made those himself too. Very fine craftmanship," he added, impressed.

"Is there anything in his pouch?" said Ellis. He pointed to the Tattooed Boy's belt. It was in shreds now, but its little pouch looked undamaged.

Carefully, the Prof loosened the leather thong that tied the pouch and took a peek inside.

"There's some dried stuff in here," he said.

"What is it?" asked Ellis.

The Prof shrugged. "Looks like some kind of plant. Maybe moss."

"Moss?" said Ellis, disappointed it wasn't more interesting. "What did he need moss for?"

"To make fire?" suggested the Prof. "You'd make sparks with a flint, first, then set your dried moss alight, then shove it under some twigs."

"Yeah, right." Ellis nodded. He knew about

making fire. Besides tracking, Gift, his African teacher, had taught him survival skills.

"Is there anything else in there, apart from moss?"

The Prof squeezed the pouch. "Can't feel anything," he said.

"Can I pick up his cloak?" asked Ellis.

"Go ahead," said the Prof. "Long as you handle it gently."

Very carefully, Ellis picked up the cloak. It felt soft and greasy, not like wolf fur at all.

The Prof said, "It must have been a spectacular garment once."

"It didn't really give warriors wolf powers, did it?" asked Ellis.

"What, the cloak?" said the Prof. "No, how could it?"

"Can I try it on?" asked Ellis.

"Better not do that," said the Prof. "We don't want to damage it."

Ellis laid the cloak, reluctantly, back on the bench.

"It's just superstition," the Prof insisted, as they left the lab. "Like all those other wolf legends."

* * *

That night, Ellis and the Prof were eating meatballs in tomato sauce with spaghetti. They were in the kitchen, in the Prof's ground-floor apartment tucked away at the back of the city's Natural History Museum. The museum was a vast, rambling building that dated back to Victorian times.

The back door crashed open and Meriel came bursting in.

"Any missions yet?" she asked.

Ellis shook his head. "Nope. No one called."

The Prof said, "It's just a quiet time. Something will come along soon."

"It better do," muttered Ellis. It was seven weeks since their last mission. They'd never been so long without one. He needed some excitement, some action.

"I need some food," declared Meriel, plonking herself down on a chair.

Meriel could have been just outside, in the garden of the Natural History Museum – there was an owl there she liked to mind-read. Or maybe she'd been up on the museum's flat roof, her favourite refuge. Or in the nearby overgrown cemetery with her feral cat friends. Or somewhere entirely different.

But the Prof didn't demand, "Where've you been?" Even though it was late and dark outside.

For the past eleven years he'd been the guardian of this half-feral girl with her extraordinary mind-reading powers. He knew a few things about her by now. He knew he had to give her freedom, or he'd lose her altogether.

He got up to dish out more meatballs and spaghetti. He was actually surprised she'd turned up for a meal. Meriel didn't live her life by the human clock. Her timekeepers were light and dark, the sun and moon and stars. Like most of the predators she admired, she was always more active at night.

Ellis wasn't so tactful. "Where'd you disappear to," he demanded, "when we went to Wolf Camp?"

Meriel gave that maddening, secretive smile. She chased a meatball around her plate with a spoon.

Ellis said, "Okay, don't tell me." Meriel exasperated him, often. She just didn't act like an ordinary kid.

But, despite that, there was an unbreakable bond between them. Meriel was indifferent to most humans. But she had a fierce, unswerving loyalty to Ellis and the Prof. Most missions would fail without her mind-reading skills. And Ellis knew, in a desperate situation, she'd die fighting to save them both. She wouldn't think twice about it. She'd do it instinctively, like a wild wolf defending its pack.

"Like your necklace," said the Prof. "Very striking. Stoat vertebrae, if I'm not mistaken?"

Meriel had them strung round her neck like beads. She seemed pleased the Prof had noticed. "Yeah, it's pretty," she agreed, clicking the white, gleaming bones together.

"Where'd you get a stoat skeleton from?" asked Ellis.

This time Meriel did answer him. "The skip," she said.

"Where?" asked Ellis.

"There's a skip down the side of the building," the Prof explained. "They're renovating part of the museum. Chucking out lots of trash, including some old specimens."

Meriel had caught her meatball. She picked it

up, crammed it into her mouth, started chasing another.

Like a dog, she was totally focused on her dinner. So Ellis carried on with what he'd been doing – which was telling the Prof about his encounter that afternoon with Nathan and the mysterious Wolf Man.

"So," said the Prof, his face concerned and serious, "do you think this boy Nathan would have hurt someone?"

Ellis thought about that. "I don't know," he said. "I don't think *he* knew either."

The Prof rubbed his scarred face. "I'm not happy with you working at Wolf Camp," he said, finally. "I don't think Scott can keep control."

"Wolf Man can," said Ellis, thinking of Wolf Man's calm hawk face and quiet authority.

"That Wolf Man's all right," declared Meriel, looking up from her bowl and wiping tomato sauce off her chin, "for a human."

Where'd she meet Wolf Man? wondered Ellis, amazed, although he knew it was no good asking her.

"I'd like to meet Wolf Man," grinned the Prof,

"if he's got Meriel's approval. Scott told me Wolf Man has a dream. He wants to reintroduce wild wolves back into this country. Up in the northern forests where they can roam free."

"Wow!" said Ellis. "I'd like to see that. Wild wolf packs back again!" He just assumed that Meriel would agree – she was a big fan of wolves. But you could never predict what Meriel would think.

She leaped up so violently that her chair clattered over, her bone necklace rattling.

Her eyes flashing fury, she roared at them, "That's stupid! Humans had their chance. Wolves were their friends once. So what did humans do? They betrayed their friends. They killed them all! Wiped them out! And now they want wild wolves again? Well, that's tough! Because they don't deserve them. Stupid, stupid humans! Spoiling everything!"

Ellis stared at her, surprised. It was the longest, most passionate speech he'd ever heard Meriel make. Meriel hardly ever used words to make a point. She preferred other means of communication, like direct action.

The Prof stayed cool. He was used to Meriel's sudden flare-ups. They lasted seconds, like a lightning strike. Keeping his voice low and soothing, the Prof began saying, "It's quite true what you say, Meriel. There's scientific evidence. Back in prehistoric times wolves and men lived and hunted together, as equals."

But the thunderclouds had already cleared from Meriel's face. Without sitting down, she grabbed two handfuls of spaghetti.

"Use a spoon, Meriel," the Prof reminded her gently. "And sit down."

Meriel gave a defiant snort, "Huh!" She didn't like chairs, or spoons. But she obeyed the Prof. She picked up her chair, crouched on it froglike and used a spoon to scoop up her spaghetti sauce.

"Okay, finished now," she said. She shoved her bowl away and leaped up, so fast that her chair clattered over again. She sucked the skin on her arm, mimicked the shrill death cries of a rabbit.

This time Travis didn't show up. Meriel shrugged. Travis didn't belong to her; he was a free creature. And he obviously had plans of his own that night. She'd have to go to the wolf enclosure alone.

"See you later," she flung at the Prof and Ellis. She darted, quick as a dragonfly, out the back door and ran off through the museum garden, leaving the door wide open behind her.

It was as if a whirlwind had left the kitchen.

Ellis carried on calmly eating his meatballs. The Prof got up and, with a quiet sigh, closed the back door and picked up Meriel's chair.

CHAPTER FIVE

Later that night, Ellis was watching TV alone in his bedroom.

He flicked through the channels. There was nothing he wanted to watch. Restlessly, he threw down the remote.

I'm bored, he thought, pacing about.

Suddenly, he remembered the wolfskin cloak, on that lab bench, down in the basement.

Why don't you try it on? a small voice whispered, inside his head. *It'd be really cool to have wolf powers.*

"That's just stupid superstition," Ellis said out loud. "It won't work."

You'll never know, will you? argued the small voice. *Unless you try it on. Go on, I dare you.*

Ellis shrugged. He had nothing better to do. And he didn't like turning down a dare, even from himself. "All right," he agreed. "But it's a waste of time."

Ellis took a key from a drawer and slipped it into his pocket. Then he left his bedroom.

Like the rest of the building, the Prof's apartment was weird and gothic. It had high vaulted ceilings and stone carvings. There were stained-glass windows in all sorts of unexpected places, sometimes even between rooms. Ellis was passing one of those windows now, just down the hallway from his bedroom. It was a magnificent round window, grand enough for a cathedral. It looked out onto the museum's Dinosaur Hall. Although you couldn't see much, through the panes of coloured glass.

The Dinosaur Hall was where Ellis was headed.

He had to walk across it to reach the stairs down to the museum basement.

A few metres past the stained-glass window was a door. It led straight from the Prof's apartment into the Dinosaur Hall. It was always kept locked so museum visitors didn't wander into the Prof's private rooms. That's why Ellis had brought his key. He unlocked the door, locked it again behind him.

He hurried across the vast, shadowy Dinosaur Hall. A life-size animatronic model *T. rex* loomed above him. There were dinosaur skeletons everywhere. They gazed at him through empty eye sockets. When Ellis had first come to live at the museum, he'd been spooked by these creepy watchers. But now he hardly noticed them.

At the far end of the Dinosaur Hall was the door to the museum basement.

Ellis had to pause there, to key in the Prof's security number. The Prof had made both his wards learn it by heart, so they could reach him, in an emergency, if he was working late down in his lab.

The basement door swung open. Stone steps disappeared into the gloom. Ellis padded down them. By day, the basement was lit up, bright as an operating theatre. But now, only night lights cast a sickly yellow glow.

It was a maze down here, of labs and storerooms and corridors. But Ellis knew exactly where he was going. He had a map of the basement in his head.

He set off, down one of the long, gloomy corridors. An octopus swam from the dark, ghostly white, its bulging eyes horribly human, its tentacles seeming to writhe.

But Ellis didn't even break step. He'd seen it often before. He knew it was long-dead, pickled in a glass tank. Just one of the ancient specimens that lined these corridors, stacked on shelves.

What's that? Ellis thought suddenly, stopping to listen.

His sharp tracker's ears had heard a muffled sound, from deep in the basement labyrinth.

He listened again, frowning in concentration. He couldn't hear anything now.

The swing doors to the lab where the Tattooed Boy was in cold storage opened with a soft *shush.* The low room was ghostly in the yellow half-light, its corners in deep shadow.

He saw the blue door, leading through to the

refrigeration room. But Ellis didn't need to go in there. In fact, he definitely didn't want to. The thought of the Tattooed Boy's mummified, mangled remains still made him shudder.

Ellis picked up the cloak from the lab bench.

He draped the leathery rag across his shoulders and waited, standing perfectly still in the deep, dark hush of the lab.

He hardly knew what he expected. He could never get as close to wild creatures as Meriel. She could share their minds, know what it felt like to *be* them. But maybe the cloak, if those old legends were true, would make him feel wolflike, just for a while.

He analysed his own feelings. Did he feel any different? More powerful? Stronger? Faster? As if he could fight a whole army?

"No," Ellis had to admit.

He closed his eyes, gave the cloak another chance.

"This is useless," Ellis decided, finally losing patience. His eyes shot open. "It doesn't work."

He felt disappointed, but only for a few seconds. Then he felt relieved, as if he'd come to his senses.

"What am I doing down here?" he muttered. He was ashamed of himself. *I need a mission*, thought Ellis for the hundredth time. It would stop him fooling around doing stupid things like this.

Then, as he laid the wolf cloak carefully back on the lab bench, Ellis thought, *Wait a minute.*

A trained tracker like him should have noticed straight away. But he'd been too focused on the cloak, too taken in by those old wolf myths.

"The Tattooed Boy's stuff has been moved about," muttered Ellis.

He remembered exactly where the Prof had put that axe and it wasn't in the same place now. The yew bow and quiver had been moved too.

Could the Prof have been back down here? Maybe. But maybe it wasn't him.

A chill passed through Ellis's body. The hairs at the back of his neck prickled. He stared around the dimly-lit lab. Then at the blue door to the refrigeration room. He saw, for the first time, that it wasn't closed. It was open, just a crack. And he knew, for sure, that the Prof hadn't left it like that. Someone had gone through that door. *Or come out.*

Once again, Ellis gazed into the lab's dark

corners. Was anyone lurking there? He tried to calm his clamouring brain.

Don't be stupid, he told himself. *That Tattooed Boy's been dead for five thousand years.*

Then, suddenly, the silence exploded. A wild ear-piercing shriek ripped through the lab and echoed into the building beyond.

What on earth's that? thought Ellis, his head whipping round.

It came from the refrigeration room, where the Tattooed Boy's body lay in its chamber.

Then Ellis realized: *It's the alarm.*

The alarm to show the temperature was rising. That the Tattooed Boy's refrigeration chamber had broken down. Or been opened...

Desperately, Ellis tried to think. The alarm wouldn't sound straight away. Only when the temperature rose to a certain level, the Prof had said. So, the Tattooed Boy's chamber could have been open for some time...

Stop it! Ellis told himself savagely. *You don't know it's even been opened. It could be just a fault in the refrigeration system.*

He tried to look round with a tracker's eyes.

Then wished he hadn't. On the floor by the bench was a blurred print. It was in some sort of grey, flaky stuff. And Ellis could see, when he squatted down to examine it, that it was the print of a naked foot.

Then his mind spun off into nightmare territory. Had the Tattooed Boy somehow come to life, escaped from his refrigeration chamber? Maybe he'd just found his things when Ellis came in, disturbed him.

Was he crouching now, in the lab's dark corners, watching, waiting to get his hands on his weapons, his wolfskin cloak?

Ellis tried not to panic. But that shrieking siren was torture. It was scrambling his brain, shredding his nerves. Suddenly, he caught a whiff of decomposition, the same smell as before, when the Tattooed Boy was thawing out.

Then, as he crouched by the footprint, he felt a hand grip his shoulder.

"Gerroff!" shrieked Ellis, pictures flashing through his brain of a withered, brown claw, with a plaited wristband.

He was conscious of a looming shape behind him. He grabbed the copper axe from the bench, raised it high above his head and spun round, ready to strike…

A strong hand seized his wrist in mid-air. A voice yelled, right in his ear.

"Ellis, it's me!"

Ellis found himself staring at a black eyepatch, a scarred face.

"Prof!"

The Prof let go of Ellis's wrist.

"Sorry, sorry," gasped Ellis, even though the Prof couldn't hear him above the alarm. "I thought you were…"

But the Prof was already limping through the blue door to the refrigeration chambers beyond.

For a few seconds Ellis stayed frozen to the spot, staring horrified at the axe still clutched in his hand, the axe that could have killed his guardian. Then he laid it, very carefully, back on the bench.

Suddenly that deafening siren stopped wailing. The Prof had switched it off.

In the echoing silence, Ellis yelled, "Prof, you okay?" He went dashing towards the blue door, just as his guardian came out.

The Prof flicked a few switches and every corner

of the lab was flooded with a bright, white light. Ellis instantly saw there was no prehistoric corpse, risen from the dead, prowling about. At least, not here in the lab.

"Is the Tattooed Boy's body still in there?" asked Ellis, jerking his head towards the blue door.

"Yes, of course it is," said the Prof.

Ellis gave a deep, shaky sigh of relief. *You watch too many zombie movies*, he mocked himself. And, anyway, what use would an axe have been against the undead?

"You didn't open the refrigeration chamber, did you?" the Prof was asking him.

"What, me? No way," said Ellis. "I just got here. I came running down here when I heard the siren."

Ellis didn't like lying to the Prof. But he was too embarrassed to tell his guardian the real truth. That he'd been down here already, trying on a five-thousand-year-old cloak, to see if it gave him wolf powers.

"The Tattooed Boy's refrigeration chamber was open," explained the Prof. "That's what made the temperature rise, set off the siren. I just closed it again. But if you didn't set it off, who did? Meriel's still out. There's only the two of us in the building."

"The Tattooed Boy's stuff has been moved," said Ellis, walking back to the bench. "I thought maybe you did it," added Ellis, not confessing to his wild imaginings about a prehistoric zombie prowling the lab.

"Not me," said the Prof. "I just got here, like you. I've been in the apartment, in my study, since dinner."

"There's a footprint here on the floor," Ellis told the Prof.

Ellis squatted down to look at it again. Now, under the bright lab lights, he could see straight away it wasn't the print of a five-thousand-year-old corpse.

"It's an adult, male," Ellis told the Prof. "Maybe two metres tall, weighs about eighty kilos. And it's all smudged. Someone was in a hurry."

"Think we've got an intruder?" asked the Prof.

"Looks like it," said Ellis.

He was all professional now, his quick eyes searching round for more clues.

"Pity there's only one footprint," he murmured.

He could have discovered a lot more from a whole set of them.

"Come through here," the Prof told Ellis, leading the way into the refrigeration room. "You may be able to pick up some more information."

The refrigeration room was small, with a low ceiling. It had four steel doors set in the wall. These were storage chambers where specimens could be kept chilled or deep frozen. One was humming softly, with winking green lights on the front. It had the Tattooed Boy inside. Ellis was pleased to see that the steel door was firmly shut.

He scanned the room, looked upwards.

"That's how he got in," said Ellis.

This part of the basement was under the museum garden. It had a window in the ceiling to let in some natural light. But the skylight had been prised open.

Ellis's sharp eyes noticed two other clues: a steel trolley wheeled under the skylight and a tiny black smear on the tiled floor, like you'd get from the rubber sole of a shoe. A picture was forming in his mind.

"Here's what I think happened," said Ellis. "The

intruder climbed over the museum wall, came through the garden, forced that skylight open. He jumped down into the refrigeration room, took his shoes off, opened the Tattooed Boy's refrigeration chamber. Then he went out into the lab, in his bare feet and was looking through the stuff on the lab bench when something disturbed him."

The Prof said, "Must have been the siren going off."

"Must have," agreed Ellis, even though he knew better. He knew *he* must have disturbed the intruder, quite a while before the siren went off, by going into the lab to try on the wolfskin cloak.

The intruder must have run back into this refrigeration room, thought Ellis. *He must have been in here all the time I was out in the lab.*

And it was only when the siren went off that the intruder had climbed back through the skylight. The wailing siren must have covered the clatter of the metal trolley being pushed underneath.

"See," said Ellis, squatting down beside the shoe print. "He put his shoes back on, climbed on the trolley and pulled himself back up through the skylight."

"Why'd he take his shoes off anyway?" asked the Prof.

"Because he was trying not to leave any tracks," said Ellis.

And he would have succeeded, if it hadn't been for that single bare footprint he'd left.

"Can't you identify his shoes?" asked the Prof.

"No chance," said Ellis, standing up. Even he couldn't do that from one tiny smudge.

The Prof shook his head, puzzled. "None of this makes any sense. Why did he break in? Why open the refrigeration chamber? Why unzip the Tattooed Boy's body bag?"

"Did he do that?" asked Ellis. "That must have given him a shock!"

"Unless he already knew what he'd find inside," said the Prof, grimly. "But the body wasn't tampered with, far as I could tell. Is anything else missing?"

They went back and checked the lab. Nothing seemed to have been stolen. The Tattooed Boy's belongings had been moved about. But they were all still there.

"Hang on," said the Prof. "Look, his belt pouch is open. I closed the drawstring, I know I did." He looked in the pouch. "It's empty. The dried moss is gone. That's what that grey stuff must be, on the floor."

"He pulled the moss out, chucked it away, then accidentally trod in it," said Ellis.

"But why take the moss out?" wondered the Prof.

"Maybe he thought there was something else in there. Something worth stealing."

"There wasn't," said the Prof. "I squeezed the pouch, remember? I would've felt it."

"My head aches," said Ellis. "This is crazy. Maybe the intruder was just some ghoul who likes being around ancient bodies."

"There's always that possibility," said the Prof. "And maybe he was just trying his luck, a spur of the moment break-in. But maybe he knew exactly what he was looking for."

"He didn't find it though, did he?" said Ellis. "'Cos nothing's missing."

The Prof shook his head, as mystified as Ellis. "If he *did* find it, I don't know what it was. But I *do* know that there's a prehistoric plant expert coming tomorrow. He's going to have a fit. There's no moss left for him to look at."

"I'll see if I can scoop some up," said Ellis. He crouched down near the bench. "Wait a minute," he said. Now the light in the lab was better, he could see something amongst the flaky grey stuff.

"What's this?" he asked the Prof.

He pointed to what looked like a small, black, spiky bead. He was about to pick it up with his fingers when the Prof said, "No, use these. Those spines look vicious."

The Prof handed Ellis a pair of long, silver tweezers. Then he took a small glass container with a screw-top lid off a lab shelf.

"Put it in here."

Carefully, Ellis picked up the tiny black object with the tweezers and dropped it inside the container.

The Prof screwed on the lid, peered through the clear plastic. He took out the pocket microscope he always carried to examine Ellis's find more closely. "It's a seed," he said, finally.

"Oh," said Ellis disappointed. "Is that all?"

"It probably got pulled out of the pouch with the moss. Are there any more down there?"

"No," said Ellis, his sharp eyes scanning the floor. "That's the only one."

The Prof put the container, with the seed inside, into his jacket pocket.

"Pity it won't grow," he said.

"Why shouldn't it?" asked Ellis.

"After five thousand years in the ice?" the Prof answered. "No chance."

The Prof took a final look round the lab. "I'll get Albert to come and fix that skylight."

Albert was the museum's ancient caretaker. He looked after the huge Victorian furnace that heated the building and did all the odd jobs around the place.

"And in the morning I suppose I'll call the police," the Prof continued. "But there's nothing else we can do here right now."

Back in the Prof's kitchen, they discussed the break-in for a while, but didn't get any closer to explaining it. Then Ellis went to his bedroom and the Prof back to his study.

Just before midnight, the Prof closed down his computer. He'd finished work for the night. As he left his study, he remembered the seed.

He took the container from his pocket and peered at the black seed. It was a strange, sinister-looking object. It was shaped like a tiny death star, with six spikes. It had a scaly coating, as if it was protected by armour.

Without thinking, the Prof tipped the seed out onto his hand.

One of the seed spikes stabbed his thumb, like a bee sting. The sudden pain made the Prof shake the seed out of his skin.

He sucked the bead of blood off his thumb.

"Ow," he murmured. His whole thumb was throbbing. You wouldn't think such a tiny seed could cause such pain. He couldn't even see it now. It had fallen somewhere among the plant pots on his window sill.

Well, it can stay there, thought the Prof. He didn't want to risk getting stabbed again. He'd search for it in the morning, using tweezers from the lab.

The Prof switched off the light as he left.

Behind him, in the dark study, moonlight came creeping through the window. It bathed the plant pots in its shimmering glow.

Hours passed and nothing happened. Except that the glow became brighter, fiercer, until the pots and the little tomato plants growing inside them seemed to burn with silver fire.

Then the soil in one plant pot heaved. It heaved again, as if something was beneath, struggling to break free. Suddenly, a tiny fist punched up through the soil. It unclenched into a grey, furry, fang-shaped leaf. Fast as a speeded-up film, more shoots and leaves burst through the soil, suffocating the tender young tomato plant.

Finally, a single fat flower bud appeared.

Five thousand years ago the slave boy, now a poor shrivelled corpse in the refrigeration chamber, had stolen seven seeds from his master the shaman. They were the shaman's magic, the source of his power. They could corrupt men, create monsters. But only when they grew and flowered. Just like one was about to do on the Prof's window sill.

CHAPTER SIX

There was a night-time prowler in the city streets. It was Meriel. She was heading for the wolf enclosure. The metro ran all night. It would have taken her almost all the way to Wolf Camp. But Meriel didn't take it. She hated riding in that clattering tin tube with other people. It was bad enough with the Prof or Ellis to keep her calm. But alone, she couldn't stand it.

So, tonight she was making her own way to Wolf Camp, by her own peculiar route. She scuttled down alleyways, like the city rats. Leaped fences like the foxes. Slunk through shadows like the feral cats. Most humans hardly saw the rats and foxes and cats who roamed their city at night. And like them, Meriel could make herself almost invisible.

It was late when she arrived at Wolf Camp, hours past midnight. The wooden cabins were in darkness. There were no signs of life at all. The Wolf Campers and Dr. Scott Spenser must all be in bed, asleep. She assumed that Nathan was safely tucked up too.

Good, thought Meriel. She didn't want anyone getting in her way. Tonight it was just her and the wolves.

She got into the wolf enclosure the same way as before, wriggling under the wire.

She was darting through the shadowy, moon-washed forest when she heard a sound. It was a very human sound, *"Harumph!"* like someone clearing their throat. And it seemed to come from above her, in the treetops.

Meriel immediately dropped flat, wriggled into

the grass like an eel. Cautiously, she parted the grass stems and stared upwards. Then she smiled.

It was Wolf Man, high above her, out on the balcony of his tree house. It was just a wooden hut, wedged in the branches.

The tree house was his main sleeping place. But Wolf Man had several smaller huts, for wolf watching and sleeping, scattered throughout the wolf enclosure. All of his huts were basic, like the one beside the clearing, where Nathan should have stayed put, but didn't. Wolf Man didn't need much to survive – just food, water, shelter and being near wolves.

Meriel watched from below as Wolf Man gazed up at the starry sky. He seemed very peaceful. There was some kind of yellow flickering flame on the balcony with him.

A candle, thought Meriel.

Its glow made a halo around his hawk face and long, silvery hair. Wolf Man wasn't going to bother her, Meriel decided. He had no idea she was there. And besides, he was too busy star gazing. Like Meriel herself, he seemed self-contained, a loner. As if he didn't need human company.

Meriel watched, intrigued, as Wolf Man blew out his candle. She could hear the wooden balcony creaking as he went back into his tree house, presumably to bed.

Then Meriel hurried on, about her own business.

"Wolves, where are you?" she whispered to herself.

It was no use trying to mind-read ravens to find out the wolves' location. The ravens would be asleep, roosting somewhere, their heads tucked under their wings.

If Ellis was here, he could have tracked the wolves. Ellis could track anything, even at night. Meriel's general mistrust of humans didn't include Ellis. She wouldn't mind if he was here beside her. Ellis was patient with Meriel and her wild ways. He didn't make her feel like a freak.

But Ellis was back at the Natural History Museum. So Meriel had to use other ways to find the wolves. Usually, she had to see an animal before she could mind-read it. That's the way it worked best. But sometimes, she could send her mind out searching and lock onto the mind of a wild creature. Especially if that creature was sending out powerful brain waves. If it was in distress in some way, maybe angry or scared or in pain.

But why should the Wolf Camp pack be in distress? They were well fed and protected here in this pretend wilderness. They didn't have to fight for survival like a wolf pack in the wild.

Meriel shrugged. Even though she didn't expect great results, or even any results at all, it was still worth a try. She didn't have all that much time; it would start getting light soon. And daylight would bring the humans out of their beds. Meriel always tried to avoid meeting humans whenever she could. She found wild creatures, even wolves, much easier to deal with.

So Meriel stood still in the dark, silent wood, concentrated and sent her mind out searching. Almost instantly she was snuffling up strong doggy smells, seeing the world not in colour but shades of grey, feeling pine needles under her paws...

"Hey! Hey, Meriel or whatever your name is!" Nathan yelled right in her ear.

Meriel stared at him. But she wasn't seeing him. Her eyes were wide open but still glazed and faraway.

"I was coming back to find Wolf Man but then I saw you," said Nathan, his thin, foxy face twisted with worry.

This time Meriel knew who he was. She'd snapped out of her trance, returned to her own body. But she swayed, almost fell. Her mind-reading sessions often tired her. But this one had left her close to collapse.

She struggled to remember. She'd located a wolf, no problem, shared its world for a few minutes. But what had happened to make her feel so physically shattered?

Then it hit her, like the shock waves of an explosion. She remembered it all. The adrenalin rush, the heart beating faster, the low rumbling snarls, the furious pacing. That wolf had been revving up for a fight. And not just a play fight between pack members – but a serious fight, for survival.

It must have been Storm I mind-read, Meriel realized.

He was the alpha male, the one who'd protect the pack if there was danger. But what danger could there be, in this wolf enclosure? Wolves were top predators here. No other creature came close. So what did Storm find so threatening?

Then Meriel remembered something else. Wolves are shy and wary. They spend their lives low down, working out how to sneak from one place to another without being seen. But Meriel remembered, when she was in Storm's brain, being high on a ridge, looking out over trees. Storm wouldn't do that unless he was checking for danger, unless he was very sure danger was close...

Nathan was really annoying her now. His chewed, jagged nails gripped her jacket. His hot breath was right in her face. He was raving, that old anger flashing out. "You got to come with me! I mean now! Like right now!"

Meriel stopped trying to remember and slid those weird, feral eyes towards him. He noticed her necklace for the first time, made of the bones of some small animal. It made her look extra freaky, like a witch doctor, or some voodoo priestess.

"Back off," she snarled, her bone beads rattling. Her eyes glittered like a cornered weasel's. She hated it when humans crowded her and hated it even more when they touched her.

Nathan instantly saw that he'd made a big mistake, trying to push Meriel around.

"Okay. Sorry. Right?" said Nathan, letting go of her sleeve. He stepped quickly away, out of her personal space. The fury in her eyes faded a little. It didn't seem that she might go for his throat any more.

Nathan felt he'd made himself look really stupid. But it was hard to break his old habits. Bullying was what he did; he didn't know any other way to behave. And it had always worked quite well – always got him what he wanted. Until the last twenty-four hours had turned his world upside down and it hadn't worked at all, not with Ellis, or Wolf Man, or the wolf pack, or Meriel.

He should have known it wouldn't work with Meriel.

Remember how cool she was, he reminded himself, *when she just came running out right into that wolf pack? She saved your skin!* She seemed to have no fear at all.

He took several deep breaths to calm himself down.

"Okay. Sorry. Right?" said Nathan again, spreading

out his hands, palm down in a peace-making gesture. "It's just that there's something wrong with the wolf pack. Sorry," he added again.

But for Meriel, the incident was already forgotten. She never bore grudges or had regrets. She asked Nathan, as if nothing had happened, "Was Storm high up, looking over the trees?"

"Yeah, he was!" said Nathan. "How'd you know that?"

Meriel shrugged, as if that wasn't important. "You didn't upset Storm again, did you?" asked Meriel. "You didn't act like you were the big boss?"

"What, me? No way!" protested Nathan, hurt at being accused. "I wouldn't do that. I know all about wolves now."

Meriel made no comment. But her disdain cut like a knife.

"Well, I don't know *all* about them," Nathan admitted. "But I do know not to do *that.* The wolves never saw me anyway. There was one of Wolf Man's hut things. I hid in it and watched them. I watched them for hours."

"So what did you see?"

"Star started dragging the cubs into a rabbit

hole, nipping them if they tried to come out. She was hurting them!"

"She was hiding them," said Meriel.

"She kept sniffing the air," said Nathan. "And growling."

So there is *danger coming,* thought Meriel. Star had smelled it, on the wind. That's why she'd hidden her cubs in a safe place.

"I don't understand it," said Nathan, raking a hand through his spiky hair. "What's got them so worked up?"

"I don't know," said Meriel. If she could mind-read Storm again, she might get more information. But she couldn't concentrate with Nathan so twitchy and anxious beside her.

Then they both heard the howl. It soared above the wood. It filled the night sky with spine-chilling echoes. As it swelled to a wild crescendo, it sounded tortured, even insane. Then it died away.

Nathan could feel goosebumps popping up all over his body.

"Was that *Storm*?" he asked Meriel, in disbelief.

Meriel didn't answer that. She'd already started running. She didn't need Nathan any more. Now she'd remembered about the ridge she knew exactly where to find the wolves.

But Nathan wasn't so easy to shake off. "Wait for me!" he yelled, crashing through the wood behind her.

In his tree house, as the howl started, Wolf Man shot out of bed. He strode onto his balcony. As he listened to that heart-stopping sound, his hawk face grew grave. When the howl was over, he scanned the wolf enclosure. From his tree house, he had a bird's-eye view.

On a distant ridge, silhouetted against a great, silver, full moon, he could see a wolf standing.

Storm, thought Wolf Man.

But it wasn't Storm who'd howled. Or Star or Grey or Dancer. Wolf Man could recognize all of their individual calls. And none of them sounded as sinister or as savage as the howl he'd just heard.

"A male wolf?" guessed Wolf Man. It had to be. No other creature howled like that. But where had it come from? It sounded close, as if it was actually *inside* the enclosure.

How'd it get in here? thought Wolf Man.

But he couldn't waste time wondering. He had to

act quickly. If it was a lone, male wolf, it would challenge Storm for pack leadership. Then Storm would have no choice – he'd have to fight. And Nathan was out there too, somewhere. Wolf Man prayed he had the sense to keep himself hidden.

Wolf Man threw on his clothes. He tied back his long silvery hair; he didn't want it getting in his way. Then he climbed down the ladder from his tree house, and went racing through the woods towards the ridge.

Meriel and Nathan were already watching the pack. The two of them crouched where Nathan had hidden before, in one of Wolf Man's beautifully built hideouts. It was a tepee, made of poles, with thick layers of moss and grass for the walls. Nathan had been lucky to find it – it was so well camouflaged that if you didn't know it was there, you'd walk straight past it.

The sky was lightening. But it wasn't dawn yet. There seemed to be no colours at all in the landscape. Everything was in stark black, or shades of misty grey. A huge pale moon still hung above them.

They peered through the spyholes in the tepee walls. There was no sign of the cubs. They must be still in the rabbit hole where Star had hidden them. Startled into silence by their mother's nips, they weren't even whimpering or whining.

Storm had come down from the ridge. He was staring into the trees, the three adult wolves lined up behind him. You could see instantly Storm was expecting trouble. His lips were wrinkled, pulled back, his teeth bared. His tail was up. The hairs bristled on his back, to make him seem as big and threatening as possible. Nathan only saw these outward signs. But Meriel knew what was going on inside Storm's head – she'd been there, just a short while ago.

A raven, that bird of ill omen, came swooping out from the trees. It wheeled overhead, a black cross in the dark grey sky.

Nathan was in a frenzy of agitation. Crouched beside Meriel in the tepee, he was chewing his fingernails ragged, until they bled. He whispered helplessly, "What's going on out there?"

"*Shhh*," said Meriel. "They might hear you."

But not a single wolf looked their way. They were concentrating on something else, gazing intently into the trees with that wide, unblinking wolf stare.

Meriel didn't have to mind-read – she could see their tension, as they stood, still as statues, stiff-legged, fur electrified, waiting for something.

Then, suddenly, in the shadows between the trees, Meriel saw two golden lights. Now the lights were moving low down, circling the pack.

Meriel breathed a low, excited sigh. She knew what was happening now – the reason for the pack's alarm. It was a rogue wolf, a lone wolf from heaven knows where, moving in on their territory.

Then the lone wolf showed itself. In an explosion of speed, that startled even Meriel, it came sprinting like a leopard through the pre-dawn haze. She got a blurred glimpse, as it streaked past, of a huge powerful body, of muscles bunching under gleaming white fur...

Then the wolf sprang on Storm. The two wolves clashed in mid-air. They crashed to the ground, locked together in a snarling, biting ball. But Storm's attacker was massive and much, much stronger. Storm didn't stand a chance.

Now the lone wolf was on top and Storm was pinned down. He snapped desperately, thrashing his head from side to side as the lone wolf tried to rip his throat. It missed his throat but tore his shoulder.

Grey, Dancer and Star circled the two fighting wolves. But they knew better than to get in the way.

Storm wriggled free, ran back up to the ridge to make a desperate last stand. The lone wolf bounded after him, its long legs eating up the ground in easy strides.

Storm's fur was wet with blood. He was flagging. He turned, panting to face the white wolf. But in one deadly pounce, it clamped Storm's head in its jaws, shook him like a rag. It seemed to have supernatural strength. Forced backwards, Storm's paws scrabbled on the ridge edge.

Nathan crawled to the tepee door. "That thing is killing Storm! We've got to do something!"

"Nothing we can do," said Meriel, hauling him back with surprising strength for such a small, slight person. "This is wolf business. Besides, it won't kill him," she added.

Wolves almost never fight to the death. Storm's attacker had done enough to show it was top wolf. It would let Storm crawl away to lick his wounds. And it would take his place.

"It just wants to be pack leader," she told Nathan.

"That's Storm's job!" said Nathan.

"Not any more," said Meriel.

In wolf world, things were simple. It was all about survival. The strongest wolf ruled the pack. Storm would be a lower-ranking wolf from now on, but at least he'd still be alive.

And at first it seemed as though Meriel was right. Everything happened as she predicted. The lone wolf didn't kill Storm or force him over the ridge edge. Instead it loosened its grip on Storm's muzzle. Storm cowered on the ground, panting, acknowledging defeat. The white wolf towered over him. With its two huge front paws holding Storm down, it threw back its head, gave a lordly, triumphant howl. That howl told the pack, *I'm your leader now.*

Nathan felt really angry on Storm's behalf. "It's not fair!" he protested. "It wasn't a fair fight!"

Meriel stared at him, incredulously. "What's fair got to do with it?" she demanded.

But then a very strange thing happened. The pack had followed the two fighting wolves up to the ridge. But instead of crowding round their new leader, licking his muzzle, greeting him, like a wolf pack should, Star, Grey and Dancer shrank back. Snarls were still rumbling in their throats. Grey darted up, sniffed the lone wolf, then backed off, growling suspiciously.

There was something about this new leader that made the pack deeply alarmed. The pack backed off further, whining, slinking behind rocks. Only Storm, too weak to escape, was still up on the ridge.

Nathan crouched, chewing his nails, frantically peering out of a spyhole. He couldn't stay still, even his face muscles were twitching. "What's going on?" he hissed.

"I don't know," admitted Meriel.

Nathan grabbed Meriel's arm, his fingers dug in. "See that?"

A fat, furry ball came waddling out of the rabbit hole.

The wolves up on the ridge couldn't see it, it was hidden from them by bushes. But Meriel and Nathan could.

Nathan dived out of the tepee door and, using the bushes as cover, went racing towards the cub.

The cub sniffed his shoe and squealed joyfully.

Nathan reached down, tried to grab it. But it wanted to play. It scooted off into the trees, expecting Nathan to chase it. Then its brother came out to join the game.

Meriel cursed. Hadn't she just told Nathan to stay out of wolf business? But now she had to act. What if the wolves saw Nathan? Things were explosive enough up on the ridge without adding humans to the mix.

She hurled herself out of the tepee in a crouching run.

Nathan was stumbling around in the wood, trying to catch the cubs. But they were too quick and wriggly. Meriel showed him how to do it. She stalked up to the pups and glared down at them with her most chilling wolf stare. Instantly, they acknowledged her as an alpha wolf. They rolled over on their backs, whimpering, showing their white furry bellies. Meriel grabbed them by the scruff of the neck, like a mother wolf would. The cubs didn't wriggle, or try to get free. They just hung limp, behaving themselves.

With one cub dangling from each hand, Meriel hissed, "Come on!" to Nathan. Nathan was going to protest. Then thought better of it. They headed back to the tepee, keeping low.

Up on the ridge, things had changed drastically. As if enraged that the pack had rejected it, the lone wolf seemed to want revenge. It rounded again on the helpless Storm, eyes blazing, teeth bared. It moved in for the kill.

The raven landed close by, in a clatter of feathers. Boldly, it hopped up, expecting a share. But the lone wolf was berserk, out of control. It whirled round, snapped at the bird with bloodstained fangs. The raven flew off, with an outraged squawk.

Then, suddenly, Wolf Man appeared at the top of the ridge, silhouetted, like Storm had been, against the moon.

Meriel gave a soft hiss of surprise: "Where'd he come from?" He must have got up somehow from the gully below.

He should stay out of it, thought Meriel.

She thought Wolf Man would have known better. In Meriel's experience, when humans meddled with wild creatures it mostly ended badly, for one side or the other.

Wolf Man stood between the injured Storm and

his half-crazed attacker. It was an insane thing to do, in Meriel's opinion.

Meriel couldn't mind-read humans. But she could guess what Wolf Man was thinking. She could guess at his strong beliefs. He was telling himself, *This wolf will back down. Wolves don't attack people*.

Meriel couldn't help wondering what the lone wolf was thinking. This was the perfect set-up for mind-reading. She could see her target; it must be projecting strong emotions. Meriel was very tempted.

Then, *No,* she told herself sternly. This was no time to go into a trance.

Besides, she could see, without mind-reading, that this was no ordinary wolf.

It wanted to kill its own kind. It didn't honour the ancient bond between wolves and ravens. It didn't seem scared, or even wary, of humans.

The lone wolf arched its back, the fur crested along its spine.

Slowly, it swung its great snarling head towards Wolf Man, fixed him with its fiery eyes. Then it sprang and hit him full in the chest. Wolf Man and his attacker went flying over the ridge edge, then vanished.

"No!" yelled Nathan.

He went racing towards the ridge. Meriel let the pups drop and raced after him.

Nathan stopped briefly at Storm. He was stretched out on a rock. Star had run back to her cubs. But Grey and Dancer came out from hiding. They began licking Storm's wounds, nuzzling him. Grey growled at Nathan, as if to say, *Keep back! We don't need you!*

Nathan stared down, horrified, into the gully. There was a river at the bottom, winding through tangles of thorn bushes and tall, bristling clumps of reeds. He steeled himself for a gruesome sight. But the lone wolf wasn't feasting on Wolf Man's body. There was no sign of the lone wolf at all. And Wolf Man was lying down there alone, half in, half out of the stream. He wasn't moving.

"We've got to get down there!" Nathan yelled to Meriel, who'd just come running up.

Meriel searched for the way down. She pointed to a steep, narrow path. "That's the way Wolf Man climbed up!"

And she and Nathan went scrabbling down it, slipping, sliding, sending an avalanche of small rocks clattering down into the gully.

"Watch out for that wolf," panted Nathan, as they skidded to the gully floor. Maybe the fall had killed it. But somehow, he doubted that. It seemed indestructible, a wolf from your worst nightmares, like the big, bad wolves of fairy tales.

"It's not here," said Meriel, with absolute conviction. She'd spotted the raven, wheeling over Wolf Man's motionless body. It wouldn't risk coming back unless it knew the lone wolf was gone.

Nathan kneeled in the muddy water beside Wolf Man, his face twisted in anguish. He'd been angry with Wolf Man before, for, it had seemed, suddenly rejecting him. But all that was forgotten now.

He risked his life to save Storm, thought Nathan. He could hardly believe it. But he'd seen Wolf Man do it with his own eyes.

Nathan's hands fluttered desperately. He didn't know whether to touch Wolf Man or not. He didn't know what to do. He'd never, ever felt so helpless.

Meriel was squatting on the bank. She didn't

have any suggestions. If humans were hurt, she always left it to Ellis or the Prof.

Then Wolf Man opened his eyes. Surprisingly, they were steady, even calm. And although he seemed badly injured, he took charge of the situation.

He grasped Nathan's arm. His voice was weak but urgent. He obviously had something important to say.

"Listen," he said. His eyes flickered to Meriel, who was watching the raven circling overhead. "Listen, *both* of you," he stressed. He paused until Meriel was paying attention. "No one must know about this. That I was attacked by a wolf inside the enclosure. It would mean the end of the Wolf Camp pack." His voice faltered. He grasped Nathan's arm tighter. "That rogue wolf must be found," he said. "It has no fear of humans. My wolves mustn't get the blame for what it does."

"I'll get an ambulance!" said Nathan.

"No ambulance," said Wolf Man, his fingers gripping tightly. "No one must know!"

Then, gasping painfully, he said something else. "I thought it was going to kill me."

"So why didn't it?" asked Meriel in her usual

blunt way. It hadn't even mauled or bitten him. Wolf Man's injuries seemed to be from the fall alone.

He raised his head, got out another word. "Water," he croaked.

Immediately Nathan thought Wolf Man was thirsty. He cupped his hands, scooped water from the river and raised it to Wolf Man's lips.

Wolf Man pushed his hand away. That wasn't what he wanted. He half raised his head, desperate to make someone understand. It was Meriel who put her ear to his lips.

"Hates…water," he gasped, his voice just a faint whisper. "Lone wolf…hates water."

"What's he saying?" begged Nathan, distraught.

Meriel shook her head. "Nothing."

Suddenly, the old man's fingers slid from Nathan's sleeve, his head fell back, his eyes closed.

"Is he dead?" said Nathan, appalled. "He's not dead, is he?" There were tears running down his face. Furiously, he tried to wipe them away, smearing snot and tears over his cheeks.

Meriel watched him, at first curiously. But then she couldn't help it, she felt a strange twinge of sympathy in that human heart she tried so hard to hide. Nathan seemed so lost, bewildered and angry. That was something Meriel identified with, caught as she was between two worlds, the human one and the world of wild creatures.

Meriel sighed, irritably. It was a big inconvenience, feeling sorry for Nathan. Now she was involved in human affairs, whether she liked it or not.

"We need help," she told Nathan. "We need to call the Prof and Ellis."

"No one must know," said Nathan, distraught. "That's what Wolf Man said! Anyway, I haven't got a mobile. Scott took it away."

"I have," said Meriel, rummaging around in her pocket. Ellis had recently given her his old one. Just in case she ever needed to call. But she'd never used it, never even switched it on.

She thrust it at Nathan. "Call Ellis," she ordered him.

"Ellis?" said Nathan. He was dimly aware that he'd heard that name before, but in his current distressed state he couldn't remember where.

"What's his number?" said Nathan.

Meriel scratched her nose. "He told me the phone knows it."

Ellis's was the only number programmed into the phone. Nathan called it and, while it was ringing, handed the phone back to Meriel. She put it, warily, to her ear as if it was going to bite her.

Meriel waited while it rang, jigging about impatiently, while Nathan kneeled next to Wolf Man, desperately trying to find signs of life. Wolf Man twitched and groaned.

"He's still alive," Nathan cried joyfully.

As if it knew there was no dinner down there, the raven overhead wheeled away.

"Hi, Ellis," said Meriel.

A surprised, sleepy voice at the other end said, "Meriel? Is that you?"

Ellis had given Meriel his old phone, showed her how it worked, even kept it charged up for her. But he hadn't thought in a million years that she would ever use it.

"Where are you?" said Ellis. "What's wrong?"

"I'm at Wolf Camp," said Meriel.

"Wolf Camp! What are you doing there?"

Meriel ignored that question. "You know you said we needed a mission?" she asked Ellis.

"Yeah," Ellis replied, puzzled.

"Well, I think we've got one."

They spoke some more. When he heard what had happened Ellis said, "I'll wake the Prof. We'll come down there. What are Wolf Man's injuries?"

"No wolf bites," said Meriel. "I think he hit his head."

"Call an ambulance," said Ellis. "We're on our way."

Then he was gone. Meriel stabbed a few buttons until the phone went dark, shoved it away in her pocket.

"Stupid phones," she muttered.

Then she told Nathan: "Ellis says call an ambulance."

Nathan bit his lip in indecision. He frowned down at Wolf Man's face. It was deathly white. His eyes were closed. But he was still breathing.

"Wolf Man said no ambulance," said Nathan. "No publicity. This all has to be secret."

"Okay." Meriel shrugged. She was a big fan of keeping things secret, away from human busybodies. "We'll sort this out on our own. Me, Ellis and the Prof."

"Hey, what about me?" Nathan protested. "Aren't

I included? And, anyway, who are the Prof and Ellis? What have they got to do with any of this?"

But, before Meriel could answer, Nathan suddenly recalled where he'd heard that name, Ellis, before...

Back at the Natural History Museum, Ellis had to shake the Prof hard to wake him up.

"Weird dreams," murmured the Prof, still half asleep. "I was running like the wind. I smelled blood."

But he soon forgot his dreams when he heard what had happened at Wolf Camp.

"Call Meriel," he told Ellis. "Tell her to run and get Scott."

Ellis tried. "She's switched off her phone!" he said, exasperated.

"Then we'd better get down there, quick as we can," said the Prof.

The Prof got dressed in a big hurry. He looked around for his jacket.

"I left it in my study," he remembered. He went limping in there to get it.

"Good heavens!" he said, astounded.

In the pot on his window sill a flower was opening. It was a small but sinister-looking bloom. Its six petals were waxy and sickly white, the same colour as pallid, unhealthy skin. It had a dark red centre, like a crimson throat.

A strange musky scent came from it, making the Prof's head swim a little.

Ellis popped his head round the study door. "Did you find your jacket?"

The Prof didn't seem to hear him. He was still staring at the peculiar plant, that had appeared, as if by magic, on his window sill.

"Shouldn't we get going?" asked Ellis, impatiently, coming into the study.

"That prehistoric seed – it must have fallen into that flower pot," said the Prof. "And look what's come up. It's already flowering!"

"Thought you said it wouldn't grow," said Ellis.

"It *shouldn't* be growing," said the Prof. "And certainly not that fast."

Then he recalled their mission. Things sounded bad at Wolf Camp. The plant would have to wait until he got back. He grabbed his jacket and hurried out of the study. "We'll take the museum truck," he told Ellis.

"Do we have to?" groaned Ellis.

The museum truck was a very uncool vehicle. It was bright red, like a toy fire engine, with *NATURAL HISTORY MUSEUM* painted along the side.

"It'll off-road better than my car," answered the Prof.

Minutes later there came the sound of the truck driving away.

Back in the quiet of the Prof's study, the flower basked in silvery moonglow. But slowly, the moonlight faded. When it did, the petals on the prehistoric flower began to shrivel. They withered into grey ash and crumbled. By the time the first sunbeam trembled through the glass, the sinister bloom was dead.

But already, another flower bud was swelling to take its place.

CHAPTER SEVEN

It was late afternoon. Ellis, Meriel and the Prof were still at Wolf Camp. They were in the cabin Scott used as an office, talking about what to do next. The bright red museum truck was parked outside.

Ellis and the Prof had arrived at Wolf Camp just after dawn. Without waking the Wolf Campers, they'd knocked on Scott's cabin door. He'd opened it a crack. Two feverish, flickering eyes peered out at them.

"I've caught a virus," Scott had told them, "I feel dreadful. It just came out of the blue."

In a few, hurried words, the Prof had told Scott about Wolf Man. "Give us the key to the wolf enclosure," he'd said. "Then go back to bed. We'll deal with this."

Scott had thrown the keys through the gap in the door. "I don't want you to catch what I've got."

The Prof had off-roaded the museum truck right to the gully. Nathan had had the sense to switch on Meriel's mobile again and give them directions.

The Prof had insisted on an ambulance for Wolf Man. Nathan had protested: "Wolf Man said, 'No ambulance!' He said, 'Don't tell anyone.'" But the Prof had been adamant. "You can't mess around with head wounds." He'd calmed Nathan down by explaining, "We can still keep how it happened secret. No one will know that wolves were involved. We'll just say he had an accident, fell off the ridge, in the dark."

Nathan had said, "What about Storm?"

But there was no time to climb back up to the ridge to search for Storm. "He'll be all right," Meriel had assured Nathan. "The pack will look after him."

"But what if the lone wolf comes back?" Nathan had asked her anxiously.

Meriel had shaken her head. She didn't know the answer to that.

Gently the four of them had loaded Wolf Man into the truck and driven him back to Wolf Camp to meet the ambulance. Nathan had climbed in with the stretcher. The ambulance men had asked him "Are you a relative?"

Nathan had replied, "None of your business," and refused to budge. So the ambulance had driven off to the city hospital, blue lights flashing, with Nathan and Wolf Man inside.

An hour ago the Prof had phoned the hospital asking for news of Wolf Man. A nurse had said, "He's still unconscious but stable." The Prof had asked about Nathan. But the nurse had said, "Who?" No one knew whether Nathan was still at the hospital, or where he was. No one but Meriel much cared.

Ellis especially didn't. "Don't care if I *never* see that creep again!" he'd declared. When they'd sat, side by side, in the truck this morning they hadn't spoken. But the tension between them had been electric.

Meriel was having a catnap, curled in the corner. She could fall asleep instantly, anywhere. The Prof was sitting at Scott's desk, resting his bad leg. Ellis was perched on top of a filing cabinet, clanging it with his heels. He was restless for some action.

Outside, it was quiet and deserted. Scott's sudden illness and Wolf Man's unfortunate "accident" made good excuses to close Wolf Camp temporarily. The Prof had sent all the Wolf Campers home this morning. It meant he and his wards could conduct their investigations in private. Besides the three of them, Scott was the only other person still here. But they couldn't count on him for help. The Prof had just been to check on him. He'd found Scott twitchy and sweating under a duvet, his face even more sickly pale, his eyes red rimmed.

"I'm thirsty all the time," Scott had told the Prof, "my skin is itchy. I'm getting these really weird dreams."

"That virus Scott caught is really vicious," the Prof had reported back to Ellis and Meriel. "The poor guy's not himself at all."

Ellis leaped off the filing cabinet, landed with a thud on the floor. Meriel's eyes shot open, instantly awake and alert. Straight away her restless energy kicked in. She sprang up and started prowling around the cabin, her fingers clicking the bones on her necklace like they were worry beads.

"So this is the situation," said Ellis. "We've got this rogue wolf, that turned up out of nowhere and muscled in on the Wolf Camp pack. And our mission is to deal with it."

"That's about it," agreed the Prof.

Meriel stopped pacing to say, defiantly, "Why do *we* have to interfere? People are always interfering. Let the wolves sort it out for themselves."

"But this lone wolf attacks *humans*," the Prof reminded her.

"And it's not just bad news for humans," Ellis pointed out. "If people find out about the wolf attack they'll go mental. They'll say, 'All the Wolf Camp wolves should be shot!'"

Now Meriel's eyes flashed ferociously. "They'd better not try to shoot Star or the cubs! They're not to blame. It's that lone wolf! It's not right in the head."

The wolf pack had sensed it. Wolves always accept the strongest wolf as alpha. But not this rogue wolf. Even after it had defeated Storm, showed it was strongest, they wouldn't accept it as their new leader.

"We might have to kill it," muttered Meriel, darkly.

"What?" said the Prof, staring at her in surprise. His ward was always passionately on the side of wild creatures. She identified with them, one hundred per cent. He'd never heard her suggest they should kill one, unless it was fatally injured and suffering.

"That might be the best thing to do," Meriel insisted. "For the wolf pack. And for humans."

"We can't just *kill* it," argued the Prof, in his calm, reasonable tones. "There is *something* wrong with it, obviously. Else it wouldn't attack people. That's not natural wolf behaviour. But it could be something that can be cured. Something simple. Like a toothache, for instance. That makes animals extra aggressive. But I'd have to examine the creature to see."

Ellis said: "That's no problem. I'll just go in there and track it. Trap it somehow. Then we can get it out of the enclosure. And you can take a look at it."

Meriel gave one of her scornful snorts. "*Huh!* You make it sound easy."

"Well, how hard can it be? It's just a wolf," said Ellis.

"It's too risky," said the Prof.

"Oh, come on!" said Ellis, exasperated.

"And it's not *just* a wolf," muttered Meriel, stubbornly. "You haven't seen it. It's a *crazy* wolf."

The Prof added, "And we don't even know if it's *inside* the enclosure. It managed to get in, we don't know how yet. So maybe it got out the same way."

"I can find out if it's still in there," declared Meriel.

"How?" said the Prof.

"I'll mind-read it." Meriel shrugged.

"How close do you have to get to do that?" asked the Prof.

"I can stand outside the fence and do it," said Meriel confidently. With a beast as powerful and aggressive as the lone wolf she'd *definitely* be able to detect its mind waves. If, of course, it was still around.

"I'll wait until tonight," said Meriel. Wolves were

always more active at night. Their mind waves would be stronger.

"Good idea." The Prof nodded.

But he was already privately thinking, *If it's not inside the enclosure, then we can't keep this secret, like Wolf Man wanted.* They'd have to inform the police, before any more people got hurt. The lone wolf roaming the city didn't bear thinking about.

"I wish we knew how it got *into* the enclosure in the first place," said the Prof.

Meriel stayed quiet. She knew it couldn't have been the same way she did, through that hole in the fence. That was far too small for the lone wolf to get through. Besides, she'd blocked it up.

"Maybe someone just left the gate open," suggested Ellis.

"Well, it's locked now," said the Prof, who'd made sure of that, when they'd driven the truck back through with the injured Wolf Man inside. "And I've given the key back to Scott."

"Do you think this wolf's still inside the enclosure?" the Prof asked Meriel.

Meriel frowned. Who knew what a crazy wolf would do next? Would it hang around? Would it go looking for another pack to lead? She took a guess. "I don't think it's going anywhere," she told the Prof. It had won its territory. And nothing would make it give it up. Not people, or the other wolves, or anything. "That wolf's a psycho," muttered Meriel. She had a very bad feeling about this mission.

"Okay, we'll plan our next move tonight," the Prof said. "After Meriel's done her mind-reading. In the meantime, we stay *out* of that enclosure."

He got up from the desk.

"I'm going to have to nip back to the Natural History Museum for a couple of hours," he told Ellis and Meriel.

He had things to do back there. He had to welcome the boffins who'd come to examine the Tattooed Boy's body. And make sure Albert had fixed that skylight, so no one else could break into the basement.

"I won't be long," said the Prof. "Call me if anything happens. And stay out of that enclosure."

"We can't get *into* the enclosure anyway," Ellis pointed out. "We haven't got the key. Scott's got it." And Ellis wasn't planning to go near Scott if he could help it. He didn't want to catch his virus.

The Prof picked up the keys to the museum truck. Ellis almost said, "I'll come with you." But in the end, he decided to let the Prof go back alone.

The Tattooed Boy had made him change his mind. Ellis didn't want to see geeky boffins, like the prehistoric plant expert, studying the boy warrior. Doing tests on his body. Pawing through his personal stuff – precious things that he'd made himself, like his bow and arrows.

Thinking they've got the right, thought Ellis, furiously. *Giving him no respect.*

"You seem annoyed about something, Ellis," the Prof commented. Ellis usually kept his emotions well hidden. That was because tracking needed a cool head. It was also, the Prof knew, his ward's way of coping with the death of his parents, just two years ago.

But the Prof could always tell when Ellis was thinking of his parents. Because he'd twist that python band on his left wrist. Round and round, until it rubbed his skin raw.

Ellis realized he'd been scowling. He altered his face, shrugged. "No, no, I'm fine."

The Prof headed for the office door. "See you two

later," he told his wards. "Don't take any risks."

Meriel shook her head defiantly. *"Huh!"*

But Ellis grinned, the anger inside him forgotten. "What, like you don't?" he mocked the Prof gently.

The Prof grinned back and changed his advice. "Don't take any risks," he told his wards, "until we've discussed them first."

On the way back to the Natural History Museum, stuck in rush-hour city traffic, the Prof suddenly remembered that mysterious flower, blooming in the pot on his study window sill.

He made a mental note: *Must give it to the prehistoric plant expert. Maybe he'll know what it is.*

CHAPTER EIGHT

Scott was in his dressing gown, peering out of his cabin window. He saw the Prof drive away in the museum truck. There was no sign of Ellis or the wild-looking girl who was the Prof's other ward.

Scott opened the window and sniffed the air with quivering nostrils.

"I smell wolves!" he growled, softly.

He padded about the cabin, scratching his skin.

He couldn't seem to stay still. The closer it got to evening, the more agitated he felt.

"Don't go into the wolf enclosure tonight," Scott begged himself. "Don't let it happen again."

But he knew it would. Events were out of his control.

He bounded into the kitchen and gulped down a glass of water. Then gulped down another.

Three hours to go, thought Scott feverishly.

He didn't even have to look at his watch. He could smell night coming. All his senses, especially smell, seemed to be super-keen.

On the window sill there were six plants growing. Each had a single flower bud. They were closed up now. But, as soon as moonlight washed over them, they would bloom into waxy white flowers with crimson throats.

They had grown from the six prehistoric seeds that Scott had taken, last night, from the Natural History Museum. Just like the slave boy, he'd meant to destroy them. But, somehow, it hadn't turned out that way.

* * *

Scott had travelled the world collecting wolf legends. A couple of years ago, a wise woman had told him the story of The Slave Boy and the Shaman. How a shaman, and his wolf-cloaked warriors, had terrorized local tribes. They'd attacked by night, more savage than wolves, killing, looting, burning. Until a slave boy, covered in swirling blue tattoos, had stolen the shaman's seven magic seeds, the source of his power.

The tribes were saved. But what had happened to the seeds? No one knew, for sure. Because the boy was never found. He disappeared in the snowy mountains.

"But, if ever you find those seeds," the old, wise woman had croaked, clutching Scott's sleeve with a clawlike hand, "you must destroy them. If they grow, they'll make men into monsters. You must destroy them, for the sake of mankind."

Scott had almost forgotten that story. Until Ellis let slip that a body was being brought to the Natural History Museum.

Could it *really* be the boy from the story? Those swirling blue tattoos made it possible. But did he have a pouch? With seven seeds inside?

I have to find out, Scott had thought.

And he had to do it alone, secretly. The scientists, including the Prof, would probably scoff at that old wolf story. They wouldn't take the old woman's warning seriously.

But Scott couldn't just dismiss it. He didn't believe in magic exactly. But some of these old stories told the truth in mysterious ways. If these seeds *did* exist there could be something deadly about them. Something that might even threaten the future of the human race.

"Then I must destroy them," Scott had decided. For the sake of mankind, just like the wise woman had said.

He felt a massive responsibility on his shoulders. But he wasn't going to shirk it. Secretly, Scott had always wanted to be a hero. And now was his big chance. Even if no one knew about it but himself.

Scott had never broken into a building in his life. But, that night, he'd found himself at the Natural History Museum. He knew the labs were down in the basement. So he'd prowled around, looking for a way in. He couldn't believe his luck when he'd found that skylight right above where he wanted to be. It had been so easy to force it open.

The first thing Scott had done, after he'd leaped down from the skylight and removed his shoes, was open the Tattooed Boy's refrigeration chamber. He had no idea that he'd tripped an alarm that would sound as soon as the body warmed up.

"No pouch," Scott had murmured. There was nothing on the poor, shrivelled corpse but a few rags and a thin, plaited wristband.

Maybe the seeds didn't exist after all. Scott began to think, *What am I doing here?*

But then he'd crept through to the lab. And there was the pouch, among the Tattooed Boy's other possessions.

Scott's fingers were trembling so much when he'd opened it, its contents had spilled on the floor.

"The seeds!" he'd breathed when he'd seen them, among the dried moss. "The slave boy didn't destroy them!"

So it was up to him to do the job. He saw a pestle and mortar on the lab shelf.

I can grind them to dust! Scott thought.

But he'd barely taken a step towards the shelf when he'd heard someone coming. Frantically, Scott had scooped up the seeds, not noticing he'd left one behind.

"Ow!" he'd gasped, as a hot tingle, just like an electric shock, fizzed up his arm. It seemed to go right into the core of his brain. He had to clutch his head for a second, he felt so weird and woozy.

He'd shoved the seeds into his pocket. His brain cleared a bit, so he'd dashed back behind the blue door and spied out through a crack. He'd seen Ellis walk into the lab, watched him try on the wolf cloak, take it off again. Scott had spotted, too, that he'd left a print of his own naked foot on the floor.

"Fool!" he snarled at himself.

At least it wasn't his shoes. He knew Ellis could identify them. That's why he'd taken them off.

Get out! his brain began screaming at him. *Save the seeds!*

But wait a minute, hadn't he planned to destroy them? Wasn't that the reason he'd broken in?

Then things had got even more bewildering. As the temperature rose, the siren had sounded, with its terrible ear-splitting shriek. In a panic, Scott had pulled on his shoes, clattered the steel trolley under the skylight, and escaped.

"You were almost caught!" he'd raged as he'd driven his car, madly, recklessly, back to Wolf Camp. But he'd got the seeds in his pocket. Now all he had to do was destroy them. For the sake of mankind, to save the world.

But their evil influence was already affecting his actions. Instead of pulverizing them to powder, he'd found himself planting them instead, very tenderly, in six flower pots on his window sill.

When they'd grown, he could hardly believe it. They were the old lycanthropous flowers of legend! He'd read descriptions of them, in many old books.

Eat one of the night-flowering blooms, the old stories said, *and you will become a wolf until dawn.*

Was that why the shaman had been so feared? Because he'd led his men on those night-time raids not as a man but transformed into a savage beast?

Cool! Scott had thought, as the heady scent had made his head reel and he'd reached out, to pluck a flower.

* * *

Scott checked again out of his cabin window. He saw Ellis go to the dormitory. He didn't come out. The wild-haired girl stayed in the office. Everything was peaceful. Time passed. Long, late afternoon shadows from the trees fell over the cabins.

"Hurry up and get dark," fretted Scott.

Then he would eat a flower and undergo a transformation. Just like he had last night, when he'd become the lone wolf and defeated Storm and almost killed Wolf Man.

He'd wanted to finish the job when he and Wolf Man went tumbling together from the ridge. But becoming a werewolf has certain conditions. Being allergic to water is one of them. When they'd hit the water, Scott couldn't bear it. The touch of it on his wolf body had been like fire. He'd swum as fast as he could to the shore.

And Scott's current sickness wasn't a virus. Like hating water, it was another result of being a werewolf. From his studies of wolf legends, Scott knew his symptoms well. When dawn comes and werewolves return to human form, they have itchy, pale skin, red eyes and are always thirsty. They have other symptoms too.

Scott turned over his hands. There they were – hairs on his palms, soft and thick, like wolf fur.

Suddenly, as he gazed at his own hairy palms, Scott was gripped by fear and horror. He thought, *What's happening to me?*

For a moment, the old Scott broke through. "I've become a monster," he whimpered. Just like the wise woman had predicted. He wasn't a true wolf – the pack had known it, last night, when they'd rejected him. He was a nightmarish wolf/man mutant. A human brain inside a wolf's skin.

"But it wasn't me!" moaned Scott. "Not really *me* in that wolf body!"

It was a Scott he didn't recognize, power-crazed, savage.

True, he'd always been secretly jealous of Wolf Man. But he'd never dreamed of doing anything violent. Until last night.

Scott moaned again with fear. He was terrified of what he'd do when he ate a lycanthropous flower and became a wolf tonight, for the second time.

"Destroy the flowers. Destroy the shaman's

magic!" Scott cried out in anguish.

But Scott knew he wouldn't destroy the flowers. He was too weak. And the lure of becoming a wolf again was too strong. Soon the old, mild-mannered, civilized Dr. Spenser had vanished again.

"Got to prepare!" Scott told himself feverishly, scratching his skin, padding about.

It wasn't dark yet. But he needed to be ready.

Scott grabbed two of the plant pots and the key to the wolf enclosure. He checked again out of the window. No one was watching. Wolf Camp was as still and quiet as a grave.

He bolted the cabin door from the inside, laid two pillows end to end on his bed, covered them with a sheet so it looked like he was sleeping. Then, still in his dressing gown, his feet bare, he slipped out of a back window with the plants.

He let himself into the wolf enclosure, locked the gate, hid the key under a rock.

His mind was razor-sharp, working at top speed. It seemed more cunning and clearer than it had ever been. And now he had no doubts at all.

Last night the wolf pack had rejected him as leader. But so what? Tonight he was going to form a pack of his own – werewolves like him. He would be in supreme power over them, alpha wolf. They would have to do his bidding.

And his first pack member would be Ellis. Scott had watched him trying on that wolf cloak. Didn't that prove Ellis was eager to be inside a wolf's skin, feel a wolf's power?

Then Scott's racing mind had another devilish idea. That bare footprint he'd left in the lab accidentally. Why didn't he turn it to his advantage? Ellis had a brilliant memory. He would remember that print. If he saw it again, like the ace tracker he was, he'd be intrigued. He'd have to follow it. Why not lure him with it, to the spot where Scott wanted him to be?

Scott laughed out loud, thrilled by his own power. He could see that his former ambitions, to lead an ordinary pack of wolves, had been pathetic. He was more than a wolf now and more than a man. He'd left other species far behind. He was some kind of super being, in a league of his own.

And when he led his own pack of creatures, just like himself, they'd be a formidable force. Nothing, no one, could defeat them. In the end, all men would become werewolves. Those that resisted would be killed.

Instead of bounding lightly on moss, Scott found a muddy path. Still clutching the two plant pots in his hairy hands, he strode along, pressing his bare feet firmly in the mud, making tracks Ellis couldn't possibly miss...

Two hours later, back in the Wolf Camp office, Meriel was staring out of the window. The sun had set, in a fiery blood-red ball. "Time to mind-read the lone wolf," she said.

"But the Prof's not back yet," said Ellis.

Ellis had been catching up on sleep in the empty dormitory, where the Wolf Campers had stayed before they'd been sent home. But he guessed Meriel hadn't slept. She'd been pacing restlessly about the office, waiting for sunset. It was obvious she wouldn't stay cooped up a second longer. Her eyes were sparkling with excitement. She was bursting to get inside that lone wolf's mind.

"I won't go into the enclosure," Meriel protested. "I told you, I can mind-read from outside."

Ellis shrugged. He didn't see any harm in that. Anyway, he couldn't stop her, even if he'd wanted to.

"I'll come with you," he said. "We'd better check on Scott first. See if he needs anything."

But Meriel didn't care about Scott. She was already darting out of the door, fast and twitchy as a weasel, her long, tangled hair flying.

Ellis took a quick peek through Scott's cabin window as he hurried past.

He's sleeping, he thought, when he saw the hunched shape under the sheet. *Good. I needn't go in.*

He caught up with Meriel by the pond.

"Is there any news about Wolf Man?" he asked her.

Meriel shrugged impatiently. "How would I know?"

"I just thought Nathan might have called from the hospital," said Ellis, "when I was catching some sleep. And anyway," he added, "don't pretend you don't care about Wolf Man. You told the Prof he was all right, for a human."

From Meriel, that was high praise. Meriel shrugged again. But Ellis knew she was shamming.

She'd been his partner on lots of missions. She'd saved his life, more than once. And although she'd never admit to human emotions, Ellis knew, for sure, she felt them.

"Wolf Man likes wolves," said Meriel. "He saved Storm when the lone wolf was going to kill him."

"Wolf Man's a good guy," agreed Ellis. "He saved *me*, when that nutter Nathan was waving that metal bar around."

"*Nathan* likes wolves," declared Meriel, suddenly.

"So what does that prove?" demanded Ellis. "That he's a good guy too? Not everyone who likes wolves is a good person!"

Meriel clamped her lips and stayed stubbornly silent. Ellis sighed. Meriel was really wise when it came to wild creatures. She probably knew more about them than anyone alive. But, in Ellis's opinion, she still had loads to learn about people. She was often as innocent as a baby where they were concerned.

"Don't be conned," Ellis advised her. "That Nathan's a creep."

But Meriel had lost interest in talking about people.

It was wolves that were preying on her mind.

She ran ahead, lightning quick. But when Ellis caught up with her again outside the wolf-enclosure fence, she was standing still as a statue. He knew it was no use talking to her when he checked her eyes. Her dazzling, defiant gaze was dimmed. Her eyes were dreamy. Her mind was out of her body, somewhere else. Had she found the lone wolf? Was she inside its head at that very moment? Ellis wouldn't know until she came back.

Ellis waited patiently in the fading light.

His eyes flickered around, checking for signs – a tracker is never off duty – when he thought, *Hang on a minute!*

He crouched down. He saw a print that was burned into his memory, that he recognized instantly. He felt the earth around it gently, with his fingertip. The footprint was very fresh, made only minutes ago.

"You might as well come out, Nathan," said Ellis. "These are your boot prints. I know you're here."

Nathan came out from behind a bush. The two boys watched each other, wary, defensive.

"What are you doing here?" Ellis asked him. "All the other Wolf Campers got sent home this morning."

"So?" said Nathan. "I'm going in to check on Storm. I got Wolf Man's permission."

"I thought he was still unconscious."

Nathan shrugged and didn't answer that.

"You can't go in if that lone wolf's in there," said Ellis. "It's too dangerous." Even he, with all his wildlife and tracking experience, would have to watch his step.

"Nobody says what I can and can't do," snapped Nathan, that old anger suddenly sparking. "Except maybe Wolf Man," he added. "Anyhow," he challenged Ellis, "how come you know all about the lone wolf? You haven't even *seen* it."

Then Meriel came back from her mind-reading trip. All Ellis's attention immediately switched to her. She shook herself like a wet dog, as if getting accustomed to being inside her own skin, seeing the world again through her human eyes.

"What did you find?" Ellis asked her.

"The lone wolf isn't in there," she said.

"You sure?" said Ellis.

Meriel shot him a scornful glare. Then she condescended to explain. "I would've found it straight away," she said.

The lone wolf was such a powerful beast. Its mind would have eclipsed all other creatures. She wouldn't even have had to search. She would've been drawn towards it, like a moth to a dazzling beam.

"Anyway, I couldn't find it," declared Meriel, her voice echoing her disappointment. "It wasn't there."

Ellis's brain suddenly grasped the implications of that. "The Prof will go ballistic. Because that means it's on the loose somewhere."

Meriel nodded. "That lone wolf is really freaky," she said. "It doesn't behave like a wolf should. I thought, if I could mind-read it, I might find out why."

Ellis nodded, sympathetically. "I thought I could trap it."

But somehow, the lone wolf seemed to have escaped them both.

"Hey!" shouted Nathan. "You two! *I'm* here, remember?"

Ellis and Meriel turned to look at him, as if seeing him for the first time. Ellis ignored Nathan's desperate outburst. He took out his mobile. "I'm calling the Prof," he told Meriel. "He needs to know about this."

It was Meriel, for once, who was more polite. "I just tried to mind-read the lone wolf," she informed Nathan.

Nathan stared at her. If anyone else had told him that, he would have hooted with scorn. But, to his own surprise, he didn't doubt her word. In fact, it would explain a lot about her. "You're telling me you can *mind-read* animals?"

"Yes, I can," said Meriel, with something like pride in her voice.

"Cool," said Nathan.

"Only I couldn't mind-read the lone wolf. Because it's not there."

"That means it's safe to go into the enclosure then," said Nathan.

Ellis said, "The Prof's not answering." Either he'd forgotten to switch on his phone, or he was driving back at this very moment. "No point in leaving a message," said Ellis. "He never checks them."

This time, *he* was ignored. Meriel and Nathan were talking about Wolf Man.

"He's okay," Nathan was telling Meriel. "They think he'll wake up soon. I came to check on Storm. See if Star needs help with the cubs. But I don't fancy getting in *that* way."

He pointed to the tree bridge, further along the fence. Its branches were sagging down, with the fence spikes poking through. "I nearly got them in my guts," said Nathan.

"You could get in how I did," said Meriel. "The way Travis showed me." She began leading Nathan along the fence.

"Where are you two going?" asked Ellis.

"To the ridge," said Meriel. "To check on Storm. See you later!"

"But the Prof said not to go inside the enclosure."

"Why not?" said Meriel. "The lone wolf isn't there any more."

Ellis swallowed any further protests. He knew they weren't going to make any difference. And he didn't want to sound boring, like a worried parent.

He just frowned, bit his lip. He was usually good

at controlling painful emotions. But he couldn't help it – he felt angry that Meriel had ignored his warnings about Nathan. Like she'd thrown them back in his face.

He felt a twist of jealousy too. It was he and Meriel who were a team. And now Nathan seemed to be trying to muscle in.

"Just who does he think he is?" muttered Ellis.

With bad feelings churning inside him, he watched Meriel and Nathan pass the locked main gate, go further up the fence, then wriggle under it.

They disappeared into the trembling shadows between the trees. Ellis knew he couldn't go with them – not that they'd asked him. Someone had to be responsible. Someone had to go back to the cabins and wait for the Prof. Maybe he'd even arrived by now.

Walking along the fence, in the direction of the cabins, Ellis thought, *I'll try phoning the Prof again*. But, before he could get his mobile out, his sharp tracker's eyes spotted something, through the fence.

It was another footprint he recognized, that he'd filed away in his memory. But this time, it wasn't a shoe print. It was a bare foot.

"The intruder from the Natural History Museum," breathed Ellis.

What was he doing in the wolf enclosure?

Ellis was torn. Should he go back to the cabins, consult the Prof? Or follow those tracks right now?

It took about two seconds for him to decide.

It wouldn't take long – they were good tracks, clear and very fresh, a tracker's dream. And he wouldn't have to watch out for the lone wolf. Meriel had been certain it wasn't inside the enclosure.

Ellis wriggled through the gap where Nathan and Meriel had got in. Roughly, he forced the wire back into place. Then he ran over and squatted down by the footprints. Immediately he was totally focused. The rest of the world was shut out.

The only thing that existed for Ellis right now was that line of naked footprints. He got out his pocket torch, shone it on the tracks. In the tiny circle of light, he could see each individual toe print, the whorls on the toe pads, as unique as fingerprints.

Who is it? he wondered. He was desperate to know the mysterious intruder's identity.

He'd soon find out. His mind sharp, his heart thumping a little with the thrill of the chase, Ellis followed the tracks into the trees...

The Prof had just arrived back in the Wolf Camp office and found no sign of his wards.

They must have set off already to mind-read the lone wolf, the Prof decided. He thought of phoning Ellis's mobile to get a progress report. Then told himself, "No." A beeping phone might distract Meriel, snap her out of her mind-reading trance.

He sat down and waited. He wasn't particularly worried. His wards could look after themselves.

He'd meant to get back before sunset and go with them. But he'd been sidelined. He couldn't escape from the boffins, wanting to discuss every detail of their tests on the Tattooed Boy.

"Did you look in the Tattooed Boy's quiver?" the plant expert had asked him.

"No," the Prof had admitted, shaking his head.

"Well, I did," the plant expert had said. "And right at the bottom I found some more dried plant material. But it wasn't moss. I finally identified it as wolfsbane," he'd told the Prof, sounding rather smug at his own cleverness.

"Wolfsbane?" the Prof had said, surprised. "Isn't that a poisonous plant?"

"Deadly poisonous," the plant expert had answered. "Ancient people sometimes carried it. They actually believed it could kill werewolves. You mix it with spit, use it to tip your arrows and shoot the werewolf with it. As the wolf dies, he changes back into human form. Sometimes, if the dose isn't too strong, the man survives. And then, apparently, he's back to normal, cured of being a werewolf for ever. Fascinating, aren't they, these old superstitions?"

"Fascinating," the Prof had agreed.

Then, suddenly, he'd noticed the time. He should have been back at Wolf Camp hours ago.

The Prof had meant to give the plant boffin the prehistoric flower in his study. But, if he did, it would mean more talking, more delay. The flower would have to wait until later.

"Sorry, must dash!" the Prof had apologized. "Got things to do..."

Now the Prof stared out of the Wolf Camp

office window. Should he go and look for Ellis and Meriel?

"No," the Prof told himself, "better to wait here."

They'd show up as soon as they'd finished and tell him the results of Meriel's mind-reading attempt.

And, after that, it depends, thought the Prof, calmly.

If the lone wolf had gone there'd be no choice. He'd have to alert the police. If it was still there, the three of them would discuss tactics. He and his wards had dealt with rogue animals before. They had to be treated with extreme caution.

But it's nothing we can't handle, the Prof told himself, sitting down in Scott's chair, resting his bad leg on Scott's desk.

Some of the papers from the desk fluttered to the floor.

The Prof leaned down to pick them up.

What's this all about? he thought, vaguely, reading a few lines.

Then he realized. It was Scott's research: the legends, stories and superstitions about wolves he'd collected for years. Here was one called *The Slave Boy and the Shaman*.

"Where does Scott find this stuff?" marvelled the Prof. "I've never heard of this legend."

But just as he was about to read it, the Prof felt suddenly guilty.

I should check on Scott, he thought. The poor, sick guy had been almost forgotten in all the drama about the lone wolf and Wolf Man being rushed to hospital.

He limped over to Scott's cabin, knocked at the door. No answer. He rattled the handle. The door seemed to be bolted from the inside. He peered through a window. In the shadows he could just see a humped shape under a sheet.

Scott's asleep in bed, he thought.

The Prof was going to leave, go back to the office. Then he squinted through the window some more. In the moon glow inside the room he saw the shape in the bed wasn't moving. Didn't even seem to be breathing, as the sheet wasn't rising and falling.

The Prof frowned. What if Scott was sicker than they thought? Had even...?

Don't be ridiculous, the Prof told himself. *Of course he hasn't died*.

He walked round the cabin and found a back window open. He couldn't climb in there with his bad leg. He came back to the front window. That shape under the sheet still hadn't moved.

The Prof made a decision. He tested the door. The bolt was loose. The Prof took a deep breath, smashed his right shoulder into the door like a battering ram. He could hear wood splinter. He did it again and the door flew open, hurling him into the room.

The Prof limped over to the bed and ripped off the sheet, saw the two pillows underneath.

"Scott!" he shouted. "Scott, are you in here?"

Then, suddenly, he caught a whiff of something. It was a strong, musky smell. He sniffed again. He'd smelled that somewhere before. It seemed to be coming from Scott's kitchen.

He hurried in there. And stared in amazement. There on Scott's window sill were four flowers, luminous and ghostly white in the moonlight. They had dark red centres. They were identical to the flower that had sprung up out of nowhere on his study window sill.

What's going on here? thought the Prof.

He had the sudden ominous feeling that this mission wasn't as straightforward as he'd thought. That there was something important that he was missing.

Could it be to do with Scott?

Unlikely, thought the Prof. Scott was a nice, decent guy. The last person you'd suspect of concealing something. So why had Scott wanted to trick them? Make them think that he was safely tucked up in bed? When he'd obviously climbed out of the window and gone somewhere...

The Prof rubbed thoughtfully at the terrible scar that ran down from his eyepatch to his chin.

He limped out of the cabin. It felt good to breathe in fresh air. That heady flower scent was making him feel most peculiar.

He went back to the Wolf Camp office and picked up Scott's research again. This time, he read *The Slave Boy and the Shaman* all the way through, his fingers rubbing at that scar, his brain making rapid connections.

He saw the similarities immediately, just as Scott had done, between the Tattooed Boy and the slave in the story.

He leafed through the pages again. He found another one, headed *Lycanthropous Flowers.*

Waxy white fang-shaped petals, the Prof read. *Red centres. Furry stems. Black, spiky star-shaped seed. Musky, wolflike scent. According to legend, they grow and flower in just a few hours, by moonlight. And those who eat them become wolves, until daybreak.*

"This is madness," whispered the Prof, when he'd finished reading.

It didn't take a genius to figure out that it was Scott who'd broken into the Natural History Museum last night. That *he'd* stolen seeds from the Tattooed Boy's pouch. The seeds that were growing now, in his cabin.

The story said seven *seeds*, thought the Prof.

He'd got one plant, growing in his study. He'd seen four plants in Scott's kitchen. So where were the other two?

What does it matter? thought the Prof.

He could believe, just about, that plants could

grow that fast. It was amazing – but not impossible. But you'd have to be crazy to think they were lycanthropous. That if you ate one they could make you into a wolf for a night.

"That *is* impossible," muttered the Prof.

But Scott obviously believed it. Else why had he stolen the seeds?

"The poor guy's having some kind of mental breakdown," the Prof decided. And, at this moment, the Prof had no idea where Scott was. He could have got into the wolf enclosure; he had his own key. And, if Meriel was right, the lone wolf was still in there. A rogue wolf that, unlike other wolves, seemed to have no fear of people. That had already attacked Wolf Man. That Meriel said wasn't right in the head.

"This could get very messy," the Prof murmured.

He got up from the desk. He'd changed his mind about sitting around waiting. His already forbidding face looked grimmer than ever. He checked his watch. It was getting late. Why weren't his wards back? Meriel had had plenty of time to mind-read. She couldn't sustain it for long. It was so exhausting, so unpredictable. Sometimes she was only inside a creature's head for a few seconds.

"I'd better go and see where everyone's got to," the Prof told himself.

He left the office, heading for the wolf enclosure.

CHAPTER NINE

Ellis followed the trail of bare footprints as it twisted between the trees of the wolf enclosure. Mostly he tracked by moonlight, only using his torch in the deepest shadow.

"Easy-peasy," Ellis murmured.

It was so easy that it flashed through his mind that whoever made these prints wanted to be tracked down.

Ellis had passed a few wolf paw prints – he'd recognized that heart-shaped pad, those four clawed toes immediately. But the prints were days old, not recent. Wherever the Wolf Camp pack was hanging out tonight, it wasn't around here.

"Got you!" breathed Ellis, scanning the ground.

He'd come to the end of the trail. The footprints led straight to one of Wolf Man's hideaways – a little round hut with a grass roof and walls made of woven branches.

For a second Ellis wondered, *Is it Wolf Man I've been following?* Had Wolf Man been the mysterious intruder at the Natural History Museum?

But Wolf Man couldn't have made these tracks. He was in the city hospital, still unconscious. And, anyway, these prints were made by someone taller and heavier than Wolf Man. Someone with a strange loping walk.

Ellis crouched in the bracken, undecided. This part of the wood was weirdly empty. No rabbits grazed in the clearings. No bats darted in crazy, zigzag flights overhead. Even the night-time predators – owls, weasels and foxes – seemed to be somewhere else. There was just moonlight and an eerie silence.

As if the wood was holding its breath, waiting for something.

I know he's in there, thought Ellis. The footprints led in. But none led out.

Ellis didn't want to confront him. That would have been stupid – he had no idea who he'd be taking on. He just wanted a glimpse. To see who'd broken into the museum, taken a peek at the Tattooed Boy's body, messed up his things.

Then, suddenly, a figure came padding to the hut doorway. It had bare feet and was dressed in a dark-blue dressing gown. It threw back its head and sniffed the air with wide, quivering nostrils.

Scott! thought Ellis.

"I know you're here, Ellis," said Scott. "I can smell you. You might as well come out."

Ellis got up from the bracken. "I thought you were asleep in your cabin. I looked through the window. I saw you!"

Scott gave a triumphant laugh. "Things aren't what they seem," he said. There was a manic, haunted look in his eyes that Ellis had never seen before.

Ellis said warily, "You're sick. You should be in bed."

Scott seemed like a changed person. But Ellis still thought, *Maybe it's his sickness that's making him act this way.* He must be out of his head, delirious with fever.

Then he noticed Scott's hands. Soft luxuriant white fur was sprouting from his palms.

Scott said, "You're wondering, aren't you, why I broke into the Natural History Museum? You're wondering what I stole."

"You didn't steal anything," said Ellis, trying to keep his voice steady while the hairs rose on the back of his neck.

"Oh, yes I did," said Scott. "And you're the luckiest boy alive. Because I've chosen you to share it."

"What are you talking about?" said Ellis.

"I'm talking about power you never thought possible," said Scott. "Not even in your wildest dreams. Power to crush anybody you choose."

"I don't want to crush anybody," said Ellis.

"Yes you do," said Scott, his pink tongue licking his dry lips.

Scott waved Ellis inside the hut with a furry palm. Warning bells were shrilling in Ellis's brain, telling him, *Just get out of here!*

But he shouldn't have stared into Scott's eyes, so hungry and hot and savage. Ellis noticed they were golden now. Hadn't they been blue before? A tracker remembered details like that.

So Ellis found himself following Scott. Inside, the hut was surprisingly roomy. Moonlight filtered through the gaps in its woven walls and striped Scott's feverish face with silver.

"Sit down," said Scott, and Ellis, hypnotized by those burning eyes, obeyed.

A strong musky scent filled the hut. As Ellis breathed it in, he felt himself getting woozy, slipping away from reality...

As if in a dream, Ellis heard Scott telling him about the Tattooed Boy. How he'd stolen seven lycanthropous seeds from his master the shaman. How, five thousand years later, Scott had stolen those seeds from the Tattooed Boy's pouch and had grown them in his cabin at Wolf Camp. Ellis crouched against the wall, mesmerized by Scott's description. The Tattooed Boy sprang to life in his mind. Ellis saw him not as a mangled corpse, but as a living, breathing hero, with his red snaky dreadlocks and blue whorls tattooed into his skin, defending himself against the shaman's warriors. Ellis imagined his wild war cry, the leather band tied tight around his wrist, the copper axe blade flashing in the sun.

Scott finished his story.

"Here they are," said Scott, reverently, picking up the two plants he'd brought from his cabin. "This is what the Tattooed Boy gave his life for."

Ellis shifted his gaze from Scott's face and stared at the sinister blooms. They glowed in the moonlight. They were deathly white, like waxy flesh. Except for their centre, which seemed to Ellis like a clot of dark red blood.

"The Prof's got one of those in his study," said Ellis.

"What?" said Scott, surprised.

"You dropped a seed," said Ellis. "We found it. It grew in the Prof's study."

Scott had been wondering what had happened to that seventh seed. "Does the Prof know what it does?" he asked Ellis. "That it's lycanthropous?"

"No." Ellis shook his head, dreamily. "Anyway, he'd never believe it."

Scott smiled a superior smile at the Prof's ignorance. He thought, *The flower's safe, for the moment.* As soon as he could, he intended to get it back. But tonight, he had more urgent things on his mind.

"Eat a flower," Scott ordered Ellis.

"Eat a flower?" Ellis repeated, like a zombie.

"Eat one and become a wolf." Scott ranted like a man possessed: "Being a wolf will set you free! You'll never feel powerless again. All that pain and anger inside you. You can turn your anger into action!" Scott's body was twitching uncontrollably. He was plucking at Ellis's sleeve. Ellis couldn't tear his gaze away from those fanatical amber eyes.

"I would've killed Wolf Man," Scott hissed, white froth showing at his mouth corners. "The water stopped me – wolves like us can't bear water. But *you* could kill Nathan."

"Kill Nathan?" The words echoed in Ellis's brain.

"I hate him too," said Scott, his eyes blazing with murderous fury. "He made me look like a fool. He showed me disrespect. We'll do it together. When we are wolves."

"Nathan's at the ridge," Ellis heard himself saying. "Checking on Storm."

Ellis's eyes followed Scott's furry palm, as it plucked off a lycanthropous flower and held it out to him.

"Eat it," said Scott. "Eat it. There's a wild wolf inside all of us. And now you can release him."

Ellis stared, hypnotized, at the flower, breathing in the scent of wolves. "Will it really work on me?" he marvelled.

"Oh yes," said Scott with supreme confidence. "It's the shaman's magic. No human male can resist it. Though only a fool would want to."

Still Ellis hesitated, torn between fear and desire.

"It will soothe the pain inside you," added Scott.

That clinched it. Ellis held out an eager, shaking hand.

It wasn't even anything to do with Nathan. He didn't hate Nathan that much. But Ellis had more anger and pain inside him than Scott could ever guess. Anger at the death of his parents two years ago, killed by poachers in Africa. Ellis had bottled it up. He was supposed to be the steady, sensible one of the team. But sometimes the hurt was unbearable. In his dazed and muddled mind, Ellis thought Scott was offering him a marvellous gift. Just what he needed to stop the pain.

He was twisting that python-skin band around on his left wrist. He didn't realize he was doing it. His dad had made it for him when he was a baby. And Ellis had never taken it off. It had grown with him, the supple skin stretching like elastic.

"See, I'll show you!" Scott was raving. The moon was bright, the flowers were blooming. Scott was itching, burning up, his body writhing with impatience. He couldn't wait a second longer to transform.

Scott thrust the flower into his own mouth, chewed and swallowed greedily.

For a few seconds, nothing happened. Then, as Ellis watched, Scott slowly bared his teeth. Four white fangs were growing from his pink gums, two at the top, two at the bottom. Scott showed his red throat and growled: "*Grrrr.*" His rank meaty breath hit Ellis full in the face.

And Ellis didn't even shrink back.

Scott's fingernails lengthened and curved into claws and fur spread, as in a speeded-up film, over the backs of his hands and up his arms. Scott's body twisted, distorting under the dressing gown as he dropped to all fours. The flesh on his face pulled out, like putty, into a long, snarling muzzle.

Then a white wolf, massive, muscular, was sharing the hut with Ellis. Its powerful shoulders rippled with ruffs and crests of fur. It was panting, its pink tongue hanging out. Ellis could've reached out and touched it. He could smell its musky wolf scent, stronger and ranker than the flowers. It stared at him with its freaky eyes – golden but horribly human. Then it bounded out of the door.

And Ellis was left alone in the hut, staring at Scott's dressing gown, in a heap on the floor, and the single lycanthropous bloom that was left.

Like Scott, Ellis was hooked in the grip of ancient forces immeasurably stronger than he was. He couldn't have resisted if he'd tried. But he didn't even want to. At that moment, becoming a wolf seemed entirely natural. Something he was born to do.

As if it was a solemn ceremony, Ellis took off his clothes and left them in a neat little pile, with his mobile and torch on top. Then he plucked the lycanthropous flower off its furry stem and ate it.

He'd expected it to taste foul, perhaps bitter or like rotting meat. But it didn't. It tasted sweet, like honey.

The first thing Ellis felt was his heart beating faster, his blood surging around his body. Curiously, he watched hairs springing out of his own skin, first a few bristles, then a thick furry coat. And there were seconds of searing agony as his bones crunched or lengthened, his tendons cracked. It seemed like his body was being ripped apart, then reassembled.

Ellis dropped to all fours, opened his mouth in a silent scream. But only a snarl came out. A young wolf, grey and lean and rangy, loped out of the hut to join Scott, his pack leader.

Together, they raced through the shadows towards the ridge. Ellis wasn't human any more. But he wasn't a true wolf either. He was that monster of people's nightmares. The wolf who's only supposed to exist in myths and stories. Who preys on humans. Who gobbled grandma and almost ate Little Red Riding Hood.

Ellis was savage power inside a wolf's skin – a hurtling fireball of rage and vengeance. With no reason, or pity or kindness. And no fear, of anyone or anything.

Sometime later, in the moon-streaked empty hut, Ellis's phone started beeping away. The Prof left a message after the tone: "Hey, Ellis. Where are you? I'm outside the main gate. Call me soon as you can. And watch out for Scott. The poor guy's gone crazy. Thinks he can change into a wolf by eating flowers!"

CHAPTER TEN

"When he's healed up," whispered Nathan, "do you think Storm will be pack leader again?"

Meriel and Nathan had found the wolves: Storm, Star, Grey, Dancer and the two cubs, in a clearing just below the ridge. Now they were sitting quietly amongst them, with a huge, neon-bright moon hanging overhead and the cubs tumbling and chasing nearby.

Storm looked much better. That ugly slash on his

shoulder, licked clean by the other wolves, was mending. He was being well fed too. There was a bloody, fresh rabbit carcase beside him. His daughter Dancer had been hunting in the woods and brought it back for him.

"Nothing to stop him being pack leader," Meriel answered Nathan, "now the lone wolf isn't here any more."

To make doubly sure it was really gone, ten minutes ago, Meriel had slipped into her trance, tried to lock onto the lone wolf's mind waves. But, like before, she'd just found a big black void. She couldn't know that the lone wolf was a mutant. A creature in wolf form but driven by human emotions. And just like she couldn't mind-read people, its mind, too, was closed to her. She hadn't picked up Ellis either. Who, at this very moment was loping in long easy strides towards the ridge alongside his pack leader, their golden eyes blazing, their long pink tongues hanging out.

"Unless," added Meriel, "Grey challenges Storm for pack leader."

"What, Storm's own son?" said Nathan. "Would Grey do that?"

"Course," said Meriel, in her usual frank way, which was so often mistaken by humans for rudeness or not caring. "Why not, if Storm's past it? But Grey wouldn't kill Storm. Not like that lone wolf tried to. Storm would just sort of, retire. But he'd still run with the pack."

"Like a much loved and respected granddad," said Nathan, reciting some words he'd seen once on a birthday card.

Meriel grinned. "Yeah, something like that."

"That'd be all right, wouldn't it, Storm?" said Nathan.

Nathan was sitting beside the injured pack leader, who was sprawled out on the grass, under the starry sky. With all the light from the moon and the stars, the sky was a weird pale blue, almost like daytime.

Nathan stroked Storm's rough coat again. He hardly dared move or breathe. He felt thrilled and privileged that Storm was allowing him to get this close.

But there was something disturbing his new-found contentment with the wolves. Something he had to get settled. "That Ellis," he said. "He's cool. He's an all right guy..."

He stuttered to a halt. He didn't know how to carry on. Meriel stared at him, gave him no help at all. She was ace at dealing with animals. But her people skills were sadly lacking. She didn't know that this was a big deal for Nathan. That this was a real, sincere apology he was trying to make.

But Nathan was determined to finish now he'd started. "Shouldn't have pulled out that metal bar. Wanted to smash someone with it. I was acting crazy."

Meriel wrinkled her nose. "You saying you behaved like an idiot?"

"Not like an idiot!" said Nathan, bristling immediately. But then he reconsidered. "Actually, yes," he said. "Yes, I did."

Star got up and stretched, lazily. She came over, touched noses with Storm, then she and Grey and Dancer padded off into the dark shadows between the trees.

"Hey, where they going?" asked Nathan.

"Hunting, probably," said Meriel. Now Wolf Man wasn't feeding them with deer carcases, the pack had to find their own dinner. Storm was left behind because he was still recovering.

"Who's going to guard the pups?" said Nathan.

It was clear that Storm was still too weak. And, the way a wolf pack works, one wolf always stays behind to babysit. Mother, uncle, brother, it doesn't matter. Raising the cubs is everyone's responsibility.

Then, suddenly, Nathan realized. It was like a dazzling light switching on in his head. "They're trusting us to do it!" he told Meriel, his voice full of wonder.

"Course they are," said Meriel, as if it was obvious. "We're part of the family now."

Nathan crawled closer to the cubs. Squealing and yipping, they bounced up, stubby tails wagging furiously. They used Nathan as an adventure playground, scrambling over his body, sliding off it, tugging and chewing at his clothes. One gripped his ear lobe between tiny, needle-sharp teeth and shook it, like a piece of rabbit skin.

"*Ow!*" said Nathan. "That hurts!"

He detached the pup carefully and put its wriggling body back on the ground. It pounced on him again like a furry football, and fiercely attacked his boot.

"You never give up, do you?" said Nathan, pretending to scold it, but all the time smiling like a proud, happy parent.

Then Storm started growling, a deep, rumbling, ominous sound. Instantly the mood changed. Anxiously, Nathan appealed to Meriel: "Is it me? Have I done something wrong?" He thought maybe he'd been too rough with the pups, even though he'd been trying his hardest to be gentle.

But Meriel said, "It's not you. Look at him."

Storm was sniffing the air, his ears laid back, his teeth bared. He rose unsteadily to his feet, gazing into the trees with that unblinking wolf stare.

Meriel said, "It's just like before, when he smelled the lone wolf."

Nathan said, "But the lone wolf isn't here any more. You said so."

So why could he feel the skin crawling on the back of his neck? He stared into the trees too. Suddenly, the friendly moon glow seemed cold and menacing. The warm, starry night grew chilly. Nathan shivered; he hardly knew why.

Then they heard the howl. It came from deep in the woods somewhere. And it was the creepiest, most blood-curdling sound they'd ever heard. It rose to a wild, desolate crescendo, then died away.

"What was *that*?" said Nathan, his eyes wide with shock.

"Could have been Storm, Grey or Dancer," said Meriel.

But, somehow, they both knew that it wasn't.

It was Meriel who acted first. She was used to trusting her instincts. Using her strong teeth, she gripped one of the cubs by the scruff of its neck. It squealed in protest. It wanted to play. But Meriel had no time to mess about. She knew danger, of some kind, was very close.

Trotting wolflike, on all fours, she dumped it into the rabbit hole that Star had chosen before for a hiding place. Meriel was galloping back for the other but Nathan was already bringing it, not in his teeth, but held, wriggling in his arms. He pushed the cub inside to join its sister.

Meriel pulled some prickly gorse over the rabbit hole.

"What are you doing?" said Nathan. "They can't get out."

"I don't want them to get out," said Meriel.

Then Star, Grey and Danger came bursting out of the dark wood, running as if demons were after them, their necks straining, their tongues lolling out, foam flying from their mouths.

They came crashing through bracken into the clearing and skidded to a stop, panting hard. Then they all turned at bay, gazing back to the woods, waiting, every nerve in their bodies alert and quivering.

Two wolves came padding out of the woods into the moonlight.

One was bigger by far than the other. Its muscles rippled under its white fur. It could rip out the throat of a cave bear, or a man, with one bite.

At first Nathan couldn't believe what he was seeing. It seemed so surreal, supernatural, as if he was trapped in some hideous dreamworld.

Then the white wolf opened its jaws wide. Nathan could see those four stabbing fangs, its other teeth designed to tear and crunch. And Nathan knew that he wasn't going to wake up. That this was for real.

"It's the lone wolf!" cried Nathan. He spun round angrily to Meriel. "You said it was gone!

And where's that other one come from?"

The other wolf was a lean, mean, grey wolf. It looked deadly and built for speed.

Meriel stared at the two wolves, amazed. But she didn't apologize. Meriel hated regrets and guilt – animals never felt them. Instead, she focused her mind relentlessly on what was happening now.

The two wolves loped closer, supremely confident, not hurrying. They knew they were top predators here.

"They'll kill our wolves!" Nathan hissed, in an anguished whisper.

The pack – run-out, exhausted – were standing in front of Storm. They faced their pursuers in a snarling, defensive line.

But Meriel had seen where the two wolves had turned their blazing eyes.

She told Nathan, with some surprise, "I think it's *you* they're after."

Nathan's reply was a strangled shriek: "What!"

"*Shhh!*" warned Meriel. "Don't move."

She watched closely, as the lone wolf raised its muzzle in Nathan's direction, sniffing the air, trying to catch his scent.

The two wolves moved to the south. But they weren't going away. They were just making a wide circle around the little wolf pack and the two humans. But all the time that wolf stare was fixed on Nathan.

"Yep," said Meriel, nodding her head. "It's *definitely* you they want."

Nathan was horrified. How could she sound so cool and casual, when he was choked with panic, barely able to breathe?

Meriel backed away a few steps. Nathan thought she was about to abandon him and go fleeing into the woods. But instead she was heading up the ridge.

"Come on," she said, shooting him a quick glance over her shoulder, her eyes as bright and feral as the wolves'.

"What are you doing?" hissed Nathan.

"You'll see," said Meriel, creeping upwards.

Now they were standing at the ridge's edge, with the rocky gully and the stream below them. Nathan could hear it through the darkness, burbling over stones.

"What now?" Nathan hissed, through teeth clenched with fear.

The two wolves had passed the Wolf Camp pack, ignoring them, as if they weren't important. They were hunting humans.

"What now?" demanded Nathan again. He was ready to take off, like a bullet, into the trees. At least there would be some cover. They wouldn't be sitting ducks like they were up here, silhouetted against the moon.

"Wait," said Meriel sharply. "They'll kill you if you run."

It was too late to run now anyway. The wolves had them cornered. They were prowling up the ridge towards them, the white wolf leading the way.

"Don't even move," said Meriel. "Just wait."

Nathan hugged himself to stop his body shaking. But he couldn't help moaning out loud. He was imagining the wolves attacking, him and Meriel crashing down onto the rocks below like Wolf Man had done.

Then the two wolves exploded into action. They came hurtling up the slope, sprinting like leopards.

"Now!" said Meriel. And she disappeared over the ridge edge.

For a few horrifying seconds Nathan thought

she'd jumped. Then he heard clattering rocks. And realized she was skittering down the same perilous path they'd used to reach Wolf Man. Nathan followed her, careering down, his boots scrabbling on loose rocks, his arms going like windmills trying to keep his balance. Then his skidding feet suddenly flew from beneath him. He bumped down the last few metres, scraping his back on the rocks and landed in a dizzy heap on the gully floor.

"Come on!" urged Meriel hauling him up.

She was wading into the stream. She was hip-deep now, like some kind of water nymph, her hands trailing in the green floating weed, her long tangled hair silver in the moonlight.

Nathan splashed in after her, his boots slipping on the slimy pebbles, the current tugging at his clothes.

In midstream they stopped. They were waist-deep.

"They're coming after us," said Meriel.

She didn't seem very surprised. The wolves were sneaking down the same path. But much swifter and more sure-footed, their great wolf paws splayed out to give them a good grip.

"We've got to move!" said Nathan. He started wading on again, slippery pebbles rolling under his feet, water weed flowing like long, green hair, tangling round his legs.

But Meriel grabbed him and said, "No, we're safer in the stream."

"What you talking about?" gabbled Nathan, pulling away. "They'll swim to get us. Wolves can kill a swimming stag. Wolf Man told me!"

"Wolf Man said something else," said Meriel. "He said he wasn't dead because he fell in water. He said the lone wolf hates water."

"I didn't hear him say that!"

"You weren't listening properly," said Meriel. But there was doubt in her eyes too, remembering those mumbled words that had come from Wolf Man's lips. Wolf Man had had a bad knock on the head. He'd been half-conscious and half-drowned. Maybe he was talking rubbish.

But Meriel was staking their lives on her hunch that he wasn't.

"It's our only hope," insisted Meriel, her lips set in a stubborn, defiant line. She knew there was no other way they could escape these wolves. In woods they might have climbed a tree. Maybe. If the wolves hadn't caught them first. But here they'd been surprised out in the open.

I should've known that lone wolf was still inside the enclosure, thought Meriel. *Then we wouldn't be in this mess.*

She shook herself furiously. That was her human heart betraying her. Trying to make her feel blame. Wild creatures never tormented themselves this way.

"Stop it!" she told her human heart, clenching her hands into fists, as if she wanted to fight her own feelings. "Back off!"

"What?" said Nathan, that old anger sparking, automatically. "You talking to me?"

It flashed through his mind how insane it was, trying to pick a fight with Meriel, when he might have only moments to live.

Then Meriel said, in a hushed voice, "The wolves are here."

"You said it's *me* they want," said Nathan. He would've liked to know *why*. But this was hardly the time to wonder. "You should go," he told Meriel.

Meriel ignored that, with an irritated shrug.

"Think they'll leave me alive?" she said. Not these crazy wolves who seemed to have a big grudge against humans.

Meriel watched them, more puzzled and curious than scared.

They were slinking to the water's edge. Would they stop? Or just plunge in and swim, sharklike, towards their prey? Meriel waited, her heart beating fast. Nathan's teeth were chattering because he was waist-deep in icy cold water. And because he was terrified.

Above them, a few shreds of silver cloud drifted across the moon.

Then, with a sigh of relief, Meriel saw she'd been right to have faith in Wolf Man. The old guy had known what he was talking about after all.

The lone wolf sniffed at the stream, dipped in its muzzle. It backed off with a growl. It shook its head. Water droplets flew sparkling from its fur like diamonds.

Then the grey wolf tried. Meriel hadn't paid much attention to it until now. It was obviously the lone wolf who was the leader.

Meriel's heart cramped inside her. The young

wolf looked just as manic as the white wolf: super-aggressive, its eyes blazing with savage fury. But did it hate water too? If it didn't, she and Nathan were in big trouble. Like Nathan said, even *normal* wolves can hunt a stag through water and kill it as it swims.

The young wolf was prowling up and down the bank, snarling. Then it seemed to make a decision. It dipped its left front paw into the water. In a cloud of spray it twisted around and sprang back onto the bank, its claws scrabbling. Yowling, it licked its fur.

All Meriel's tension was released in a great hoot of laughter. In the middle of the stream, she and Nathan bumped fists in triumph.

"We can escape," said Meriel. "Long as we stay in water."

She glanced back at the young wolf, still furiously licking its paw. It was in a pool of bright moonlight, its grey fur tinged with silver.

Suddenly, Meriel felt a jolt of recognition inside her.

Nathan was already wading upstream. He and Meriel had had a lucky break. Now they had to get away, fast. He was absolutely sure that those two wolves were killers. That they would never, ever give up the hunt.

"Come on!" he urged Meriel urgently. "We've got to move!"

Why was she standing still, gazing back at the bank?

He waded back to her. "Come on!"

She pointed with a trembling finger. "That other wolf," she said. "It's got Ellis's wristband! Look, on its left front leg!"

"What?" said Nathan, bewildered. Clouds were over the moon again. He strained to see in the grey light. The white wolf was prowling up and down the bank snarling, its white fangs flashing in the shadows.

Then the clouds scudded away. And Nathan saw the band, round the leg of the young wolf. A band with a black and gold pattern.

"How do you know it belongs to Ellis?" Nathan demanded. "Lots of kids wear wristbands."

"Not like that," said Meriel. "It's python skin. They had this tame python in their house in Africa. It caught the rats. And when it died, Ellis's dad made him a wristband out of its skin. And then, after Ellis's parents got killed—"

"What?" interrupted Nathan, not sure he'd heard right.

"Ellis's mum and dad got murdered, by poachers, just over two years ago."

Nathan stared at her. "Murdered?" he repeated, stunned. He'd somehow thought the softly spoken and grave-faced Ellis was a lucky, privileged kid, who'd had it easy all of his life.

It flashed through Nathan's head, *I got him really wrong.*

But there was no time to think about that, because Meriel, so cool, even indifferent before, seemed to have totally lost it. She yelled at the grey wolf. "What did you do to Ellis?"

She flung herself forwards into the water, began a furious doggy paddle. And Nathan realized, horrified, that she was heading *towards* the two wolves. They stood on the bank, expectantly, tongues hanging out, jaws open, as if they were laughing.

"No!" roared Nathan.

He grabbed Meriel by the back of her jacket. She went under and came up spluttering, splashing and fighting. She was lashing out wildly, trying to hit him. With open palms, he blocked her blows.

"Ellis never takes that band off!" she screamed.

She whirled round, shrieked at the wolves. "What have you done to Ellis!" She was struggling through the water again, towards the wolves.

Nathan didn't know what to do. He grabbed her round the waist, lifted her clean off her feet and began to haul her through the water to the opposite bank. He thought she'd fight him every step of the way. But she suddenly went limp, floated on her back, her eyes staring up at the stars. He dumped her on the bank and sat beside her, done-in, water streaming off him, head drooping between his knees.

He stayed like that a long, long time. When he came to his senses, his first thought was: *You shouldn't have got out of the water!* As long as they stayed in the stream they were safe. Maybe the wolves could get across somehow...

Nathan raised his head. His frantic gaze searched the opposite bank. At first he thought his eyes were playing tricks. The wolves weren't there. The stars had faded, the sky had lightened to a pale pearly grey. In the east the clouds were fiery. It was dawn.

"They've gone!" he said, joyfully. Meriel lay in a soggy heap beside him. Her wet, tangled hair hid her face.

"They've gone!" he told her again. "I can't believe it!"

Meriel pushed her hair from her face. Had she been crying? It was hard to tell whether it was tears or stream water. But she wasn't fighting like a wild cat any more. All the fire seemed to have gone out of her.

"They've killed Ellis," she said dully. She was sure that's what had happened. It was the only way they could have got his wristband. Though she couldn't account for how it got tied to that wolf's leg.

But one thing she knew for certain. "They're not real wolves," said Meriel. "They're monsters."

Nathan closed his eyes. He only meant it to be for a few seconds. But he was so shattered, he fell into a deep slumber.

* * *

When he opened his eyes again, the sun was blazing high in the sky. He stared at it groggily.

Then he suddenly realized. *It's late morning. I must have fallen asleep!*

Meriel was asleep too, on the bank beside him, curled up like a dog.

As soon as she felt him move, her eyes shot open. She seemed to be awake immediately.

"Let's get out of this place," she said, springing up.

"We should check on the wolf pack first," said Nathan.

But Meriel was already wading to the bank. So Nathan followed her. He had to move fast to catch up.

On the way back, Meriel said nothing at all. She seemed to be shut in on herself. She stumbled behind Nathan through the wolf enclosure, her face white and stony. Ellis would have recognized the signs. He'd have known that look meant trouble. That Meriel was seething inside, that she was going to do something reckless and unexpected. But Nathan couldn't tell what she was thinking – he hadn't known her long enough for that.

Nathan kept checking behind them. But he and Meriel weren't being hunted. The two wolves' evil presence seemed to have vanished from the wood. Birds were singing, flitting from bush to bush. Warm, golden light flooded through the trees. It was a lovely, sunny day. Everything seemed ridiculously normal. Nathan was even beginning to ask himself, *Did last night really happen?*

Then he walked out of the trees and saw the Prof outside the wolf-enclosure fence, sitting hunched up by the main gate.

"Hey!" yelled Nathan. "Hey, Prof!"

The Prof struggled to his feet, hobbled towards the wire. His usually forbidding face looked haggard and anxious. He was limping badly. He'd spent hours walking around the perimeter fence, trying to find his wards.

"I fell asleep," admitted the Prof, looking ashamed.

"You're not the only one," said Nathan.

"How'd you get in there?" the Prof asked Nathan, through the wire. He hadn't even known Nathan was back at Wolf Camp, let alone inside the enclosure. "And where are Ellis and Meriel?" the Prof demanded.

"I don't know where Ellis is," said Nathan, "but Meriel is right here behind me."

In a torrent of words, he began telling the Prof about their night of terror. "We went in to check on Storm 'cos we thought it was safe to go in 'cos Meriel couldn't mind-read the lone wolf but then it turned up with a new wolf and they went for us, and Meriel said, 'It's you they want,' and she said to jump in the stream, so we did but then Meriel said this new wolf was wearing Ellis's wristband and she went ballistic and said they'd killed him..."

Nathan came to a stuttering halt. The Prof didn't seem to be listening. He was gazing beyond Nathan into the trees.

"Where's Meriel?" asked the Prof.

"I *told* you!" said Nathan. "She's right..." But when he turned around, his words trailed away into confusion.

There was no one behind him. Without him noticing, Meriel hadn't followed him out of the trees. Instead she'd slipped away, back into the wolf enclosure.

"She's gone!" shouted Nathan. "She was there last time I looked!"

"Can you get out of there?" asked the Prof.

Nathan ran along inside the fence, wriggled under it where he and Meriel had got in, and raced back to where the Prof was waiting.

"Did you say there are *two* rogue wolves now?" asked the Prof, looking seriously worried.

"Yes," said Nathan, nodding frantically.

He was about to start blurting out his story again. But the Prof rested both his hands firmly on Nathan's shoulders.

"Look at me," said the Prof.

Nathan's eyes had been flickering everywhere. He focused them on the Prof's scarred face. And felt himself calming down.

"Right," said the Prof. "Just take it nice and slowly. Start at the beginning again and tell me *everything* that happened last night."

CHAPTER ELEVEN

Ellis woke up, alone, back in the hut. He felt terrible, shivering one minute, burning up the next, like he'd caught the flu. He ran his tongue around his dry lips, rubbed at his sore, red-rimmed eyes.

His skin itched. He scratched frantically at his chest. Then wondered, vaguely, why he had no clothes on. They were in a neat pile on the floor, his phone and torch on top. He pulled on his jeans and T-shirt just for warmth, didn't bother with his trainers.

He poked his head out of the hut door. The sun dazzled him. With a whine, he crawled back into his dark den, sat slumped against the wall, in a dreamy, feverish trance.

He stared curiously at his own shaking hands. They didn't seem to belong to him. He turned them over and noticed, on his palms, soft grey fur was growing.

Ellis licked the fur. And suddenly a flashback slammed into his head – of loping through the wood behind his pack leader. He felt the thrill of his own savage strength, of knowing he was feared by all living things. He'd killed a rabbit in one second, snapped its neck. He could still taste its blood in his mouth. Then he'd gone hunting for bigger prey...

That's all he could remember about being a wolf. But those few details were more real and vivid to him than anything happening now.

His whole body ached to feel that kind of power again. In his agitation, he twisted the golden and black python-skin band on his wrist. But it wasn't his dead parents he was thinking of. It was being a wolf. It was the only thing that mattered, the only thing worth living for.

He stared hungrily at the two lycanthropous plants. Two flowers had been eaten last night. But now, each plant had a new swollen flower bud, just waiting to blossom. Ellis could remember eating his flower, how sweet it had tasted on his tongue. And how, afterwards, his muscles and bones had been cracked and wrenched and twisted. He remembered excruciating pain. But that pain seemed like a blessing because it would free him from this puny human body and give him the wolf form he craved so much.

"Soon," Ellis promised himself. "Soon."

To give his jittery hands something to do, Ellis reached out and grabbed his phone, checked his messages. He heard the Prof's voice, telling him to beware of Scott.

Ellis knew it was his guardian. But no emotion crossed his face as he listened. The voice from the phone seemed to come from a dreamworld. A world he wasn't part of any more. Only his wolf life was real to him now. And only his pack leader worthy of his respect and loyalty.

Ellis pulled back his teeth, gave a wolfish grin. It amused him that the Prof thought Scott was crazy.

He'll soon learn, thought Ellis with satisfaction.

Scott's dressing gown was gone from the floor. But Ellis didn't feel abandoned. He knew his pack leader would be back tonight.

Ellis hurled his phone out of the hut door. It represented a world he wanted nothing to do with. Humans, all humans, were his enemy now.

He licked his cracked lips, had one more mad scratch at his itchy chest. Then closed his eyes and waited for nightfall.

Outside the wolf enclosure, Nathan had finally finished telling the Prof his story.

The Prof shook his head. "What's going on here?" he asked himself.

He blamed himself for not keeping a tighter grip on things, for spending too long at the Natural History Museum, listening to boffins.

He had the same sinister thought as before – that there was something behind all this he hadn't taken account of. Something causing havoc, making animals, people, even his wards, behave in bizarre, unpredictable ways.

"This mission is getting out of control," muttered the Prof.

He had no idea where Ellis had got to. Or Scott, with his crazy werewolf delusions. And Meriel, it seemed, was out for revenge. She'd gone back into the enclosure, convinced that something bad had happened to Ellis and those two rogue wolves were responsible.

It wouldn't matter to Meriel that they weren't like ordinary wolves. That they were vicious and had no fear of humans. Meriel didn't calculate risks or consequences. She was like a fierce little terrier who attacks a Rottweiler.

First things first, thought the Prof. He needed to go in there and get Meriel out. Before she found the two wolves, or they found her.

Maybe he'd find Scott in there too. And what about Ellis? The Prof wouldn't allow himself to think about his ward being hurt or killed. He pushed that to the back of his mind.

You don't even know if Ellis is in *the enclosure,*

he told himself, *let alone that he's been attacked.*

But what about that wolf Meriel saw wearing his wristband?

Stop it! the Prof told himself, trying to calm his wild imaginings. *Don't go there! Meriel must have made a mistake.*

He checked his watch. "It's afternoon!" he said astonished. "We've wasted so much time!"

He started limping back towards Wolf Camp.

"Where are you going?" said Nathan, running after him.

"I'm going to get the truck," said the Prof.

He was desperate to get into the wolf enclosure. He planned to use the truck to smash down the main gates, then off-road it through the woods to find Meriel.

But, as he hurried past Scott's cabin, a thought struck him: *Scott has a key!* It was a slim chance. But if Scott hadn't gone into the wolf enclosure, maybe he'd left his key lying around somewhere.

The Prof burst into Scott's cabin. There was a hunched shape in the bed. That was the pillows of course. But then the Prof thought, *I can't remember pulling that sheet back over the pillows.*

And then the shape in the bed twitched. The Prof strode forward and ripped off the sheet.

"Scott!" he said.

Scott had come back. He lay curled up in his dressing gown. He was shaking and shivering. He didn't look any better. In fact, he looked worse.

"Where have you been?" the Prof demanded in a voice that he meant to be sympathetic but instead was full of suspicion.

Suddenly Scott uncurled. He turned his head on the pillow. His eyes had been mild and pale blue before. Now they were golden fires. And they blazed with such savage triumph that the Prof staggered back.

"I've been leading my pack," said Scott. He raised his head proudly and sniffed the air at the memory.

The Prof was still trying to grasp what was happening. "For goodness' sake, Scott," he burst out. "Surely you don't believe this werewolf rubbish?"

"Look at his hands," whispered Nathan, who'd followed the Prof into the cabin.

The Prof leaped forward and grabbed Scott's hands. Scott didn't resist, just wore the same lordly, arrogant smile, as if the Prof could do nothing to stop him now.

"There's fur growing on them," said the Prof in an awed voice. He noticed too, how Scott's nails had grown into thick, yellow claws.

Scott drew back his lips. His four canine teeth poked out, two top, two bottom. They were long and sharp, like wolf fangs.

"It's the shaman's magic," said Scott. "Its power has endured for five thousand years."

The Prof's scientific mind was racing, struggling to find some logical explanation.

It was Nathan who said, "He's got the lone wolf's eyes." Nathan could remember those eyes, burning into him, when he'd been shivering last night, waist-deep in the stream.

Nathan pointed a shaky, accusing finger at Scott. "That white wolf, it was you, wasn't it? You, all the time!"

The Prof was staring at Nathan, as if to say, *Are you crazy too?*

But Nathan had no trouble believing it. For him, it was a kind of relief. It let normal wolves off the hook. It proved they had no connection at all with this freaky wolf/man. Meriel was right when she'd said, "It's a monster."

But even she hadn't guessed the mind-boggling truth.

"So who was that grey wolf?" Nathan asked Scott. "The one that came with you last night?" Even as Nathan asked the question, he remembered that python wristband and realized he already knew the answer.

"It was Ellis, wasn't it?" said Nathan.

The Prof loomed over Scott, who was still crouched on the bed.

"Where *is* Ellis?"

"In the wolf enclosure," Scott answered the Prof. "Waiting for nightfall."

"*Where* in the wolf enclosure?" asked the Prof, making his voice more threatening. He grabbed Scott by his dressing gown collar but let him drop in disgust when he got a blast of that meaty breath.

But Scott told him without being forced. He described the location of the little hut, how he'd fooled Ellis into tracking him there, then convinced him that being a werewolf would soothe the pain inside him.

The Prof was still bewildered about what exactly had happened to Ellis. He assumed that Scott had brainwashed Ellis somehow.

"How *dare* you mess with my ward's mind!" said the Prof, his voice soft but shaking with fury.

Then another possibility occurred to the Prof.

"Did you make Ellis eat a flower?" he demanded urgently.

He didn't believe they could really change you into a wolf. But some plants could make you hallucinate, imagine all sorts of weird things.

But Scott wasn't listening to the Prof. Now Nathan had guessed his secret, he just couldn't stop talking. It was a massive buzz, boasting about his werewolf powers. Scott thought nothing on earth could stop him now. That he was far beyond the reach of feeble mortals. Like mythical heroes, werewolves are invincible. Hardly anything can harm them.

Scott was still raving, describing how werewolves would conquer the world, when the Prof hobbled towards the kitchen. He went inside and closed the door behind him.

Minutes later, a grinding engine started up.

It got faster, rose to a nerve-grating whine.

Scot faltered and stopped, gazed towards the closed kitchen door. "What's he switched my juicer on for?" he asked Nathan.

Then a terrible suspicion hit him. *"No!"* he screamed. He went flying towards the kitchen door, crashed through it.

The Prof was just feeding the last of the four lycanthropous plants from Scott's window sill into the juicer. Furry stems, fang-shaped leaves and fat buds were being whizzed by the blades into grey sludge. The sludge was rippled with creamy and crimson streaks from the unopened flowers.

Scott screamed, "No!" again, hysterically. He tried to attack the Prof, but the Prof fought him off with one hand while he poured the grey gloop into the sink, turned on the tap and watched it swirl down the plughole.

Scott seemed to collapse completely. He crumpled onto the floor in a quivering heap.

In all his bragging, he'd kept one thing secret – the source of his werewolf powers. Ellis had said that the Prof had grown the seventh seed in his study. But that he had no idea it was shaman's magic.

It looked like Ellis was wrong.

Nathan was watching from the door. "What are you doing?" he asked the Prof, bewildered. "What's going on?"

"I'm destroying these plants," said the Prof. "According to legend you eat a flower and it turns you into a wolf. Just for one night."

"So that's how you do it," said Nathan, astounded.

The Prof shook his head. "Only in fairy tales! Okay, maybe Scott did eat a flower. And it caused those wolflike symptoms, hairy hands and the rest. Lots of plants contain powerful chemicals. Some can affect your mind and body. But *none* can turn you into a different species!"

Scott raised his head. "How did you know?" he asked the Prof, in a quavering voice. "How did you know about the shaman's magic?"

The Prof didn't answer that – didn't tell Scott he'd read his private research. He just said, "Where are the other plants?"

Scott shook his head, dumbly.

"I know there are seven," said the Prof. "I've just turned four into soup. So where are the others?"

he demanded, carefully not revealing that there was one blooming, right now, in his study at the Natural History Museum.

Scott's head drooped. He seemed to have lost all hope. The fire was gone from his eyes. He twisted his hairy hands in despair.

"I'll find them," said the Prof. "And when I do I'll destroy them. I'll destroy every single one. That should put an end to this dangerous nonsense. But first," declared the Prof, "I'm going into the wolf enclosure to get Ellis and Meriel."

"I'll come with you," said Nathan.

"No," said the Prof. "Someone's got to stay here. Make sure Scott doesn't go anywhere. He's sick, not responsible for his actions. Can you do that?"

Nathan frowned. He didn't want to stay with Scott. He wanted to be back in the wolf enclosure, where all the action was. He felt that's where he belonged. And wasn't Wolf Man counting on him to look after things?

It was on the tip of Nathan's tongue to protest, start making a scene. But then he looked, really looked, at the Prof's face. He could see that the guy was seriously worried about his wards.

Just keep your mouth shut for once, Nathan, he ordered himself.

"Sure, I'll stay," he told the Prof.

Scott seemed like a broken, defeated man. "I'm going back to sleep," he said. He could barely crawl back to his bed. He seemed to have about as much strength as a newborn kitten. He pulled the sheet right over his head and hid from the world.

"It's like babysitting," said Nathan, contemptuously.

"No, I don't think he'll cause you any problems," the Prof agreed. "And thanks, thanks for your help. I mean, this is our mission – no reason you should get involved."

"I was already involved," said Nathan, rather hurt that the Prof should think he wasn't.

The Prof was going to ask Scott for the key to the wolf enclosure, but then he saw it, beside the bed. He grabbed it and limped hurriedly to the door. "I'll be back," he told Nathan, "as soon as I've found Ellis and Meriel."

"Better find Ellis quickly," advised Nathan, giving the Prof a significant look. "Before sunset, I mean."

The Prof left the cabin and, five minutes later, Nathan heard the museum truck roar by, heading for the wolf enclosure.

Huddled under the sheet, Scott heard the Prof drive away. His eyes sparked with fire again, his cunning mind was working at top speed. He hadn't realized the Prof knew about the shaman's magic. When the Prof found the two plants in the hut, he'd destroy them. Scott had no doubt about that. The Prof was a man of his word.

Scott had no doubt, too, that when the Prof got back to the Natural History Museum, he'd destroy the seventh plant.

That's why Scott was determined to get to it first.

Nathan paced the cabin, restlessly. He was bored already. He thought, *Wonder if there's any food in the kitchen?*

Then, just at that moment, a feeble voice mumbled from beneath the sheet, "Nathan, could you get me something?"

"What?" demanded Nathan. The Prof had said Scott was sick, not responsible for what he did. But Nathan had no pity at all for him. That lone wolf had almost killed Storm and Wolf Man. It would have killed him and Meriel, too, if it could have.

"What do you want, you freak?" Nathan couldn't help saying.

"Can I have two paracetamols?" quavered Scott from under the sheet. "My head really hurts."

Good, thought Nathan. He couldn't help grinning. Last night Scott had been a savage beast, fearless, with terrifying powers. But now he needed two paracetamols for his headache.

He's really gone to pieces, thought Nathan as he went into Scott's tiny, windowless bathroom. *Back to his old pathetic self*. He'd never had a very high opinion of Scott in the first place.

Nathan didn't see that behind him, a fur-covered hand, with long yellow talons, was sneaking out from under the sheet.

"Where are they?" yelled Nathan, searching the bathroom cupboard. He couldn't see any headache pills.

Suddenly, he heard something bumping and scraping across the floor. *What's that?* thought Nathan.

He was going to investigate when the bathroom door slammed, shutting him inside.

"Hey!" said Nathan, startled. He tried pushing at the door, but it only opened a crack. There was something blocking it.

Outside, using brute strength he didn't know he possessed, Scott rocked the heavy wardrobe that last half metre, jammed it right up against the door frame. Now the door wouldn't open at all.

"Hey!" came Nathan's enraged, muffled voice from inside. "What are you doing out there? Open this door!"

He looked wildly around the bathroom. There were no windows.

"Come on, Scott, let me out!" he yelled.

Nathan hammered on the door, punched it with his fists in frustration. He couldn't believe he'd let himself be trapped so easily, that he'd believed Scott was beaten.

He stopped pounding the door when his knuckles began bleeding. Then he yelled himself hoarse. But no one came to his rescue. Finally, he realized it was useless. Wolf Camp was deserted. He'd have to wait until the Prof came back. He lowered the toilet lid and sat down on it, with his head in his hands.

Scott hadn't taken his car – he'd only get stuck in city traffic. Instead he was running with a tireless steady lope towards the Natural History Museum and what could be the last lycanthropous plant in existence.

He took backstreets and alleyways. A chef from a Chinese takeaway was putting out rubbish in his wheelie bin. He saw a wild man bounding towards him. He had hairy hands. He was panting like a mad dog, his tongue hanging out. The chef dived back into his takeaway and bolted the door.

Scott stopped, threw back his head and sniffed the air with flared nostrils. He could smell night coming.

"Soon," he promised himself. "Soon."

Trapped in Scott's tiny bathroom, Nathan took his head from his hands. His dull eyes scanned the room, the walls, the ceiling. Then, suddenly, he had a brainwave. He leaped up onto the toilet seat. The ceiling was made of cheap, polystyrene tiles. Nathan punched one out. Above it, he could see only blackness.

"Yay!" Nathan gave a whoop of triumph, but softly, in case Scott could hear him.

Just as he'd hoped, the bathroom had a false ceiling. That dark space above must be the cabin loft. If he could get up there, he could crawl through. There were only two other rooms in the cabin – the kitchen and the living room that doubled as Scott's bedroom. There must be a trapdoor down to one of them.

Nathan punched out a second tile. It flew up into the roof space. He drove his fist into another. It crumbled and polystyrene chunks rained down.

"Just punch out a couple more," he decided.

Then there'd be a hole big enough for him to haul himself through and escape.

CHAPTER TWELVE

Meriel's body bounced and rocked on a pillow of rising air. The *swoosh* of rushing wind filled her ears. The black feathers on her back were as glossy as polished jet.

Nothing surrounded her but empty space. Below her the earth curved. She hung for a moment, floating, her tail and wing feathers fanned out for balance.

Then she banked, tilting one wing, and swooped down over the treetops of the wolf enclosure. Her sleek head turned this way and that, scanning the ground. *There!* Something large and shiny red flashed in the blurry green mass. Her quick raven's eyes fixed onto it. She gave a harsh, warning croak, *"Kerrark!"*

And then, with a shuddering jolt, Meriel was back inside her own human body.

For a few seconds she felt dizzy, disorientated. Then she gave a deep, soulful sigh. It always shocked her, this abrupt change. To be flying free one second, with the whole sky as your playground, then to be snatched from the heavens, dumped back in your human body. Rooted to the ground again like a tree.

Then Meriel forgot her sense of loss. She hadn't been flying for pleasure. She'd been mind-reading the raven to try and locate the two rogue wolves. She hadn't found them. But there'd been something – something odd – about what she'd seen below her.

Meriel struggled to recall it. To interpret with her human brain what she'd seen through the raven's eyes. She remembered something red. Ravens can see red really well. They can see more shades of red than humans. They can spot a wolf kill from high in the sky. And tell, by the colour of the blood, whether the kill is recent, or days old and hardly worth scavenging.

But this red wasn't a bloody wolf kill. Meriel sighed with relief about that. This red was too bright and gleaming, all in one solid block.

Suddenly Meriel worked it out.

"The museum truck!" she breathed. That moving red splodge was its roof, as it bumped and lurched through the wolf enclosure wood.

So the Prof was searching for Ellis too. Or what was left of him.

Meriel snarled softly. There went her human brain tormenting her, showing her terrible visions. Ruthlessly, she shut it down. Relying on animal instinct alone, she raced through the trees like a greyhound. She had one purpose in mind – to intercept the truck and team up with the Prof. Although she'd never admit it, she desperately needed his reassuring presence.

The Prof stomped on the brake. The truck screeched to a halt.

"Meriel!" he gasped, his eyes wide with horror.

She'd just shot out of the trees right in front of him. He'd nearly knocked her down.

"Hello, Prof," said Meriel, climbing into the truck's long front seat, beside the Prof.

The Prof's hands were still gripping the steering wheel, his face grey with shock. He took several deep breaths to calm himself. It was absolutely no use yelling at Meriel. She'd have no idea that she'd almost given him a heart attack.

"I think those two wolves got Ellis," said Meriel, bluntly. "I don't know how. But one of them had his wristband on its leg. Ellis wouldn't give that up. Not unless..." Meriel stopped. She didn't usually shy away from speaking the truth. But now she found she couldn't go on.

The Prof nodded. He knew what that wristband meant to Ellis. But then he put Meriel out of her misery.

"Ellis isn't dead," he said.

Meriel said nothing. Just sat tense, her bony hands clenched into knots, her face white and grim.

"Did you hear me?" the Prof asked, gently. "I said Ellis isn't dead."

Meriel crumpled in the seat. The message had finally got through. Her face flooded with relief. The Prof had never seen Meriel cry. But this time, he thought she might. He put a hand out to comfort her. But she shied away, like a wild pony. The Prof drew his hand back. You could only go so far with Meriel. She didn't like human contact.

"But he's in serious trouble," added the Prof.

Meriel sat up straight again. Her eyes took on their usual fierce gleam. "What kind of trouble?" she asked.

"I don't know exactly," the Prof admitted. Then, in clear, simple words, he told her what Scott had told him.

"So *that's* why I couldn't mind-read the white wolf!" said Meriel. "'Cos it was a wolf with a human brain! And that grey wolf with the wristband was Ellis all the time!" Meriel chuckled. She seemed tickled pink by that.

The Prof stared at his ward. "Not you as well! *You* don't *believe* all this magic stuff do you? That eating those flowers *really* turns humans into wolves?" For the Prof, just *thinking* about it turned his scientific world upside-down.

But for Meriel it was a massive relief. It made *her* world normal again. Those rogue wolves had thrown it all into chaos – they weren't like any creatures she'd ever encountered. And now she knew why.

"*Course* I believe it," she told the Prof, cheerily. "Now everything makes sense!"

The Prof shook his head and sighed. "I'm glad you think so."

He started up the truck. They went jolting again down the rough track between the trees. The wood seemed to be getting denser. The Prof had to slow to a crawl. Time ticked by. Their progress was maddeningly slow.

"I could've walked faster," grumbled the Prof.

"Let me out!" said Meriel, twitching beside him.

"No," said the Prof. "This time, we stay together."

Finally he stopped, switched off the engine.

"According to Scott, the hut is around here somewhere," he told Meriel. "Scott said Ellis would be inside, waiting for nightfall."

The Prof glanced out the truck window, up through the trees.

He cursed under his breath. The sun had gone down without him noticing. The sky had changed from blue to grey. Then he saw the moon. It was just a pale disc at the moment, sketched in the sky. But soon it would grow brighter, stronger.

"There's the hut," said Meriel, pointing out a grassy roof rising from behind some tall purple foxgloves.

"Right," said the Prof, opening the truck door. His scarred face looked grimmer than ever. He was steeling himself for what he'd find in there. He had no idea of the state his ward was in.

"I'm guessing those other two plants are in there with Ellis," he told Meriel. "We *must* destroy them. But Ellis won't like that," added the Prof, thinking of Scott's reaction. "He'll fight us. He'll cry and beg—"

Meriel interrupted, "Let me go in first."

The Prof turned to her, surprised. He was about to repeat, "No, we stay together." But then, suddenly, he reconsidered. He knew there was a bond between Ellis and Meriel. Going on missions together had deepened it. *Maybe*, the Prof reasoned, *she can deal with this better than I can.*

So he told Meriel, "Ten minutes. I'll stay in the truck for ten minutes. Then if you haven't brought him out, I'm coming in. Your first priority is to destroy those plants. They're the cause of all this trouble."

Meriel pushed her way through the purple foxgloves. She knew those lycanthropous plants had to be destroyed. But she didn't want to see Ellis crying and begging.

She thought, *There must be another way.*

She didn't have a plan in her head. But Meriel never did. She always trusted her instincts. When the right moment came, they'd tell her what to do.

She didn't call out to Ellis. She just marched straight into the hut. It was gloomy inside. Then she saw Ellis, huddled against a wall.

"Hey, Ellis," she said, "it's me, Meriel."

Ellis looked like a freak. His grey eyes, usually calm and steady, glowed with a spooky gold light. They were hungry, haunted. They flickered everywhere. His pink tongue poked out constantly, licking dry lips. Meriel noted that he had his python wristband on. And that his palms were grey and furry.

He seemed pleased to see her.

"You're just in time," he greeted her. As he said that, a frail sliver of moonlight came trembling in through the hut doorway, started sneaking over the floor towards the two plastic pots containing the lycanthropous plants.

Meriel glanced at them casually, then squatted down beside Ellis. The moonlight flickered briefly on the stoat vertebrae round her neck, made them gleam. Then it crept on.

"So what's it like," Meriel asked Ellis, "being that grey wolf? I mean, I'd really like to know. 'Cos I can only mind-read wolves. I can't *be* one. Not like you can."

Ellis's sickly white face flushed with self-pride. He leaned close, like he was sharing a secret. She smelled his wolf breath. Ellis was usually modest, slow-speaking. But now boastful words poured out of him, with fanatical zeal.

"It's like the best thing ever," he gloated, his eyes gleaming. "You're invincible. King of the world! Nothing can touch you! Every living thing bows down to you! Even ordinary wolves. 'Cos ordinary wolves are pathetic," Ellis confided, "compared to us."

Meriel nodded, gravely, as if she agreed. Her ten

minutes were ticking away. She had no time to argue, or persuade. And anyway, words had never been her weapon of choice. She didn't trust them, deceiving you, messing with your mind. Action was what she believed in.

"We're looking for more wolves like us," Ellis was raving. "Brother, sister wolves. Want to join our pack, Meriel? It's easy. Just eat one flower."

He stared, greedily, into the shadows. And just as he did so, the moonlight spilled into the plant pots. Immediately the fat, grey buds split open. Waxy white petals uncurled from inside, revealing the flowers' crimson throats. A musky smell filled the hut.

Mmmm, wolves, thought Meriel, taking a second, deeper sniff.

"It's time," said Ellis, reverently. "Go on, eat one," he urged Meriel, just as Scott had urged him.

Meriel thought, *I've got about five minutes*. She closed her eyes, let her animal instincts decide. Her eyes shot open again. She knew what to do.

"Okay!" she told Ellis.

She pulled the plant pot towards her, ripped out

the whole plant and crammed it into her mouth with both hands. She chomped away for a bit, then swallowed it, leaves, stem, flower and roots.

She wiped some red flecks of flower off her lips.

"Welcome, wolf sister," said Ellis, eager for Meriel's transformation to start. Then he'd eat the flower from the second plant. The white wolf would come to fetch them. Together, they'd run through the woods like the pack from hell. And heaven help any living creature, man or beast, who got in their way.

Ellis waited.

Nothing happened. Meriel stayed Meriel – the same slight girl with the dark, tangled hair and those freaky, feral eyes.

"It's not working," said Ellis, in stunned disbelief.

Meriel shrugged. "I'll try again."

She tipped out the other plant, mashed it to a green pulp between her teeth. Then gulped it down, just like she gobbled her dinners.

"It's the shaman's magic," Ellis told himself, parroting what Scott had told him. "No human male can resist it."

Then his golden eyes narrowed, suspiciously. Something had only just occurred to him.

"Wait a minute," he said. "You're not a human male. You're a human girl!"

"Don't remind me," said Meriel, scowling. It wasn't being a girl she minded. It was being human she hated admitting to. "Anyway," she said, "it obviously doesn't work on girls."

She was very relieved about that. Her instincts had told her it wouldn't. She hadn't felt drawn to the plant like Ellis; hadn't felt its power at all. But instincts can sometimes be wrong.

"Besides, I don't need your stupid magic, do I?" declared Meriel. "I'm fierce enough already." And she bared her sharp, white teeth at Ellis, in a wolfish grin.

Ellis stared at the empty plant pots, the soil dumped on the ground.

"Hey!" he yelled, at last waking up to what she'd done. "You've destroyed both plants!"

Meriel thought, *Here it comes!*

She'd managed to stop Ellis begging and crying like a baby. But she couldn't stop him going ballistic. She got ready to run. If she led him outside, the Prof would grab him, bundle him into the truck.

But the storm never came. Meriel stared at Ellis curiously. He was still sitting against the hut wall. He wasn't in a rage, trying to rip her head off. He seemed meek and gentle as a lamb.

"The Prof's outside with the truck," said Meriel. "You coming home with us?"

"Yes." Ellis nodded eagerly. "I want to come home." He sprang to his feet and loped outside after her.

The Prof was just climbing out of the truck. Meriel's ten minutes were up. Then he saw his wards coming. He stared, amazed. It was obvious that Ellis had eaten a flower last night – he had the same physical symptoms as Scott: the hairy palms, twitchiness and all the rest. But Ellis wasn't fighting mad as Scott had been when the Prof had destroyed the four plants in his cabin.

The Prof thought, anxiously, *Maybe Meriel didn't find the other two plants. Maybe she didn't manage to destroy them.*

But when Meriel reached him, she gave a thumbs-up sign. "No more plants," she said.

"You've destroyed them?" said the Prof, in disbelief. "Both of them?"

"Yep," said Meriel, as if it was no big deal. She climbed into the truck.

The Prof stared after her. He had no idea what she'd done inside the hut. But she seemed to have worked some kind of miracle.

The Prof threw his arms around Ellis, gave him a crushing bear hug. "You'll be all right now, son," he said, forgetting for a moment that he wasn't Ellis's real dad. "You'll be all right. Get into the truck. We're taking you home."

"Home," repeated Ellis.

He climbed, eagerly, into the truck's front seat, beside Meriel.

Back at the Natural History Museum, moonlight spilled through the window in the Prof's study. It crept along the sill where the only lycanthropous plant left in the world was waiting. Tonight, as if it knew it was the last hope for werewolves, it bristled with flower buds. The moonlight fell on them. They opened together in all their sinister red and white glory. Their musky wolf scent filled the study, drifted down the empty corridors of the museum.

There was no way it could have reached the truck that was rattling down a grassy track in the wolf enclosure. But still Ellis seemed to smell it. Sitting beside Meriel, he sniffed the air, gave a wolfish smile. His golden eyes sparkled with cunning.

"How do you feel, Ellis?" said the Prof, briefly switching his gaze from the windscreen to glance at his ward. The Prof's face was full of anxiety. Ellis had hardly said a word since he'd climbed into the truck. The Prof wondered what he was thinking. He wondered, too, when Ellis's weird physical symptoms would go away – the hairy palms, the changed eye colour. The Prof was trying to stay calm, but his mind was tormented by concerns and questions.

This mission isn't over yet, he thought.

He still couldn't explain those two rogue wolves who'd somehow got into the wolf enclosure. The idea that they'd been Scott and Ellis was just beyond bizarre. Even though Meriel and Nathan seemed to have no problem believing it.

It's no good, I just can't, the Prof decided.

Ellis was still locked into brooding silence. And Meriel wasn't talking either. So the Prof said, forcing his voice to sound normal, "You two must be starving hungry! What about sending out for pizza when we get home?"

They reached the wolf-enclosure gates. The Prof got out of the truck to open them. Drove through, locked them again behind him. Then he drove to Scott's cabin. He stopped the truck outside.

"Wait here," he told Ellis and Meriel. "I'll just be a second."

He limped in, shouting, "Nathan. It's me!" In one glance he saw Scott's empty bed, the big, heavy wardrobe jammed against the bathroom door.

"Nathan!" he yelled more urgently.

A figure came crashing down from the ceiling. Startled, the Prof leaped back. Nathan staggered to his feet. He was filthy, covered in cobwebs and dead flies and beetles' wings. He'd been crawling through the pitch-black roof space, feeling around with his hands.

"I found the trapdoor," he said, gazing above him at the square hole in the ceiling.

"What happened?" asked the Prof.

Nathan said, "Scott got away. The creep went and trapped me in the bathroom!" Already Nathan sounded angry, defensive, as if he was sure the Prof was going to blame him.

But the Prof said, "I'm sorry, Nathan, it's my fault. I shouldn't have left you alone with him. I thought he wouldn't be any trouble."

"He was like a crazy man!" said Nathan. "He shifted that whole wardrobe by himself!"

The Prof felt again that he'd been one step behind on this mission. That, somehow, he'd totally underestimated the forces he and his wards were up against.

"Where do you think he's gone?" asked Nathan, brushing spiders' webs out of his hair.

"I think he's gone to find another lycanthropous flower," said the Prof. It seemed those flowers were highly addictive. That once you'd tasted one, you'd do anything to get another.

The Prof's mind was racing madly, trying to think where Scott might go.

Would he head for the wolf enclosure, go back to the hut where they'd found Ellis? "But he must know I'd destroy any plants I found there," the Prof murmured, thinking aloud. Then an alarming thought struck him. "Did Scott find out about the plant in my study?" the Prof asked himself. "*I* didn't tell him. But what if Ellis did?"

"What plant in your study?" said Nathan. "What you talking about?"

But the Prof was already hurrying out to the truck. Meriel was prowling around, stretching her legs. She hated being cooped up. The Prof poked his head into the truck. "Ellis," he said, "does Scott know about the lycanthropous plant in my study?"

"I didn't tell him," said Ellis. But there was a superior smile playing around his lips. And the Prof had to remind himself that this wasn't the Ellis he knew. That, since he'd swallowed the flower, his ward's personality had totally changed.

Meriel seemed to agree. She tugged at the Prof's sleeve. "Never trust a werewolf," she hissed into his ear.

The Prof leaped into the truck. "Come on," he said to Meriel. "I think we'd better get back to the Natural History Museum, fast as we can." He was suddenly certain that Scott was heading there.

Nathan had followed the Prof out to the truck. The Prof told him, "Hop in."

"No," said Nathan. "I promised Wolf Man I'd stay here, keep an eye on the wolf enclosure."

The Prof had forgotten about the wolf enclosure. That was a worry he could do without. But could Nathan be trusted? The Prof frowned. "That's a big responsibility—"

"You saying I can't do it?" interrupted Nathan. He felt sick with despair. He'd found something good at last. And now it was being snatched away.

Typical, thought Nathan bitterly. *That's the story of my life!* He didn't know how to deal with his crushing sadness. And what about his promises to Wolf Man? That old anger lashed out. "You know what you can do?" he spat at the Prof. "You can—"

Meriel shot Nathan a killer glare, as if to say, *Shut up!* With a superhuman effort, Nathan swallowed his rage. It felt like stones going down his throat.

"What do you think, Meriel?" the Prof asked his ward.

Meriel thought about it. She looked Nathan

critically up and down. "I think he'll do a really good job," she said, finally. "The wolves trust him, like they trust Wolf Man. Nathan's part of their family now."

"That's good enough for me," said the Prof. "Okay, Nathan, I'm leaving you in temporary charge until Wolf Man comes back. Call me if you need any help. Here's the key."

The Prof handed over the key to the wolf-enclosure gate. As he took it, Nathan felt his lower lip trembling. He bit it savagely with his teeth to stop it. Then, "Thanks, Prof," he said, struggling to keep his voice casual.

"What's the hold-up?" came Ellis's angry voice from the truck. "I need to get home!"

"We're going right there," said the Prof, climbing in and starting up the engine.

The truck pulled away. Nathan waved. He gave Meriel a grateful grin for being on his side, for speaking up for him.

But, as if it embarrassed her, Meriel stared out of the windscreen and pretended not to see.

As the Prof drove his wards through the city, he felt glad all the boffins studying the Tattooed Boy would have left the museum and be safely at home by now.

He didn't want them in any danger.

He had an ominous feeling that Scott wasn't going to be easy to deal with, that he'd fight like a demon to get that last plant.

I wish we'd never found that seed, thought the Prof.

He couldn't believe something so tiny and ancient could cause all this violence and suffering.

They stopped at a red light. The Prof drummed his fingers on the wheel, waiting for green. Meriel was curled up like a cat in the footwell, having a quick snooze. Ellis was slumped against the truck window, his face turned away.

The Prof couldn't see the secret, wolfish smile on his ward's lips, couldn't hear what he said because of the engine noise.

"Soon," Ellis was murmuring to himself. "Soon."

CHAPTER THIRTEEN

Scott vaulted over the iron railings, into the garden of the Natural History Museum. He landed springily on bare feet. Last time he'd come, only two nights ago, to steal the seeds, he'd had a real problem climbing these railings. It had taken him several tries to haul himself over. And he'd landed, clumsily, in a heap on the other side.

Scott snarled softly.

"How things have changed," he gloated. Even in this human form, he was unrecognizable from his old self. The new Scott thought, *He was so weak, so feeble.*

He padded through a shadowy garden, crunched along a moonlit gravel walk. He could see the grand entrance to the museum now, with its wide stone steps and marble columns. There was no one around. The museum was closed and deserted. Scott padded round the side of the building. There was no red museum truck in the car park. That meant the Prof was probably still at Wolf Camp.

But Scott didn't care if the Prof was there or not. Nothing, no one, was going to keep him from taking that lycanthropous plant. It belonged to him.

"I'm the rightful heir of the shaman's magic," Scott told himself. He felt he'd been specially chosen.

Scott was almost at the skylight – the one he'd used before, which led directly down into the refrigeration room, where the Tattooed Boy's body was stored.

But first he had to get past that gigantic metal skip again. The same skip where Meriel had found her stoat skeleton. It was overflowing with all sorts of junk chucked out during the museum renovation.

A tall mirror was leaning against the skip. It had been magnificent once. Its frame was carved with bunches of grapes and cherubs. But now its frame was cracked, the mirror blotched with mildew. But as Scott loped past, the moonlight suddenly caught the glass, made it glow with a silver light.

Scott turned and saw his own reflection.

His eyes widened with shock. For a few seconds, the old Scott resurfaced.

Who's that? he thought, leaping back.

There was a stranger in the mirror, wearing a dressing gown. A stranger who looked like the living dead. His gangling limbs were twitching and shivering. His face was as white as a ghoul's, apart from his red-rimmed eyes. As Scott watched, horrified, a pink tongue slid out, licked dry lips. The stranger's golden eyes stared back at him: cruel, arrogant and utterly without pity.

The stranger lifted a fur-covered hand to scratch at his itchy flesh.

And, suddenly, Scott realized he was doing the same.

Awful realization struck him. He was looking at his own reflection. He gave a ghastly moan. "That can't be me," he whispered. "What's happened to me? What have I become?"

He reached out a trembling hand and touched the glass, as if to make sure it wasn't someone else. But then the mirror started to topple. It crashed to the ground and shattered into hundreds of gleaming splinters. Scott couldn't see the monster in the glass any more.

He stood for a moment, appalled and bewildered, his mind in chaos.

But then his head lifted, his nostrils flared. His keen sense of smell had caught a whiff of something. He sniffed deeply, sniffed again, then growled with satisfaction. The musky wolf scent of the lycanthropous flowers was luring him. It had drifted along corridors, seeped through ventilation grills to find him.

In that instant, the old Scott was buried again, as if he had never been.

The new Scott began breaking in through the skylight. He gave a scornful smile at the caretaker's feeble attempt to keep him out.

Albert had nailed the skylight down and put a metal grill over the top. But that was child's play for a werewolf. Scott wrenched the grill off and ripped out the skylight, leaving a gaping hole. He slid through it, let himself drop and landed, soft as a panther, on the white tiled floor of the refrigeration room.

His sharp eyes scanned the small space. It was just like before, when he'd broken in: the dim yellow night lights, the low hum of machinery. There were the four shiny steel doors to the refrigeration chambers. Only one was in use, the lights on its control panel flashing green.

Inside it was the Tattooed Boy.

Suddenly, out of nowhere, an image slammed into Scott's mind of what he'd seen, two nights ago, when he'd opened that door, searching for the shaman's seeds.

He pictured again in his head the Tattooed Boy, shrivelled to the size of a five-year-old child, his stick limbs twisted and broken, his face so badly mashed that even his own mother wouldn't know him.

And suddenly pity flooded Scott's mind – a pity for humans he hadn't felt since he'd first tasted the lycanthropous flowers.

"That poor boy died for the seeds," Scott told himself. "The shaman's magic killed him."

Scott snarled softly and shook his head, as if to chase away that picture, those thoughts that troubled and confused him.

He padded across the tiles, opened the blue door into the lab. Here the musky scent of the plant was stronger. His human feelings fled away. He felt like a werewolf again, cruel and pitiless. Hunger burned inside him. And only one thing would satisfy it – eating a flower and transforming into his wolf shape.

"The plant is in the Prof's study," Scott told himself. Now all he had to do was find it.

Scott smiled and bared his four pointed teeth. Nothing on earth would stop him reaching it – no locked doors, no puny humans. He'd attack, without hesitation, anyone who got in his way.

"Soon," Scott murmured to himself, as he loped past the lab bench where the Tattooed Boy's possessions lay neatly arranged – even his wristband which the boffins had managed to prise off.

The experts had been studying them all day. They'd been busy making notes, labelling things.

And on one label, stuck to the lid of a little glass dish, Scott saw a word written: *WOLFSBANE*.

Scott shrank back, as if from flames. He gave a low rumbling growl. He knew, from his research, what wolfsbane was. It was deadly poison. According to the old legends, it could kill a werewolf, if he either swallowed it, or got shot by an arrow tipped with it.

Furiously, Scott lashed out with a hairy hand, to sweep the dish off the table, let it smash on the floor. But the Tattooed Boy's fine copper axe got in his way, seemed to leap up at him as if it were alive. Scott's palm was slashed open. After five thousand years, the axe was still razor sharp.

"Owwww!" yelled Scott. He didn't expect to feel such pain. Werewolves, even in their human form, think they're invincible, not frail and weak like ordinary mortals.

He stumbled around cradling his bleeding hand, found a towel, wrapped it tightly round, like a bandage.

This shouldn't be happening! he thought, as a red stain spread, even through the towel.

He leaned against a bench, clutching his

bandaged hand. For a few seconds, his shock at the pain made the old Scott surface.

Stop this! the old Scott urged him. *Before you hurt anyone else!*

Scott turned his anguished face towards the lab bench. He knew these precious sane moments wouldn't last long. The lure of the shaman's magic was too strong, too powerful.

"No one else must get hurt because of me," Scott whispered desperately.

He had to do something, act *now* or this chance would be gone for ever.

He stared at the wolfsbane. His mind was a dark swirling chaos. But then he had one thought that sliced through his torment like a laser beam.

"Wolfsbane," he told himself. "It's the only sure way. The only way to save the world from *me*."

As he reached for the glass dish his hand was shaking. But beneath the old Scott's mild manner, there'd always been steely courage. Ellis had witnessed it when Scott had rushed out, without a thought for himself, to try and disarm Nathan.

Scott found that courage now. He grabbed the box with his uninjured hand, opened it. Sprinkled some wolfsbane into its glass lid. The wolfsbane had been ground to a green powder by the Tattooed Boy's own hands. He'd prepared it to tip his arrows, in case the shaman himself pursued him.

Scott had no idea how much was a fatal dose. He sprinkled some more.

That should do it, he thought.

Before he could change his mind, he quickly spat into the powder, mixed it to a paste with the Tattooed Boy's dagger.

He was going to swallow it. Then he had a much better idea. If the poison went straight into his bloodstream, it would act more quickly. It seemed to Scott that the long-dead Tattooed Boy had somehow arranged all this. That he was reaching out across five thousand years, helping Scott to free himself from the shaman's magic.

Once Scott would have thought that was crazy. But, after what he'd been through, nothing seemed impossible.

He unwrapped his bandaged hand and, wincing, pressed the wolfsbane paste into the wound. It stung like crazy. He waited for it to take effect.

As he waited, Scott's wild, frantic eyes gazed at

the lab bench. It seemed as if all of the Tattooed Boy's short, tragic life was there, laid out on display, for boffins to paw over. Like he was just some frozen prehistoric specimen. Like he'd never been a living, breathing human being.

And suddenly Scott was desperate to do something. One last thing before he died. It seemed vitally important. He wanted to thank the Tattooed Boy, personally, for helping him escape from the werewolf's curse.

Scott didn't notice how his limbs were getting cold and heavy. He concentrated all his failing strength on his final task. He staggered into the refrigeration room. He was finding it really hard to breathe. All his muscles seemed paralysed; his heart was slowing down. Fighting to get air into his lungs, Scott slumped against the Tattooed Boy's refrigeration chamber.

He could feel his brain shutting down and blackness descending.

Open it, Scott ordered himself. *Open it!*

There wasn't much time. With his last remaining strength, Scott pulled down the lever and opened the steel door. The trolley slid out easily on its metal wheels. Scott fumbled at the zip on the body bag.

He saw the bald, coconut-sized head, a stick-thin arm. Scott seized the boy's claw hand for a moment and clasped it.

"Thank you, my friend," he managed to gasp. "For saving me."

Then his knees buckled. He held onto the trolley for support. His eyes closed and he crashed to the floor, face down.

For a while, nothing happened in the refrigeration room. Eerie yellow light lit up the scene. Everything was quiet and still. The Tattooed Boy's body lay frozen on its trolley. Scott's body lay, unmoving, on the floor.

Then very slowly, the Tattooed Boy started to thaw. His temperature rose, one degree, two...

Suddenly the alarm was tripped. It tore the silence apart. It shrieked down the gloomy basement corridors of the Natural History Museum. It shrilled out into the night, through the open skylight. You could hear it even in the car park, where a red truck was just pulling up, with the Prof and Ellis and Meriel inside.

"What's that noise?" said Meriel, instantly awake. She uncurled from the footwell and slithered back onto the front seat of the truck, beside Ellis.

"What noise?" asked the Prof. He knew Meriel, like a dog, could hear higher-pitched sounds than other humans.

He opened the truck window, switched off the engine.

"I can hear it now," he said, his face grim. "It's the alarm on the Tattooed Boy's refrigeration chamber."

"So?" shrugged Meriel. "What's that mean?"

"I don't know," the Prof admitted. It could be simply a technical fault. Or it could mean Scott was already in the building.

Ellis gave a secret smile at the Prof's confusion. He was pretending to be asleep. But he'd never felt more alert. He sniffed the air. The musky smell of wolves drifted through the truck's open window. That meant the lycanthropous flower was in full bloom, waiting for him. He was frantic to reach it. It was hard to stop his body writhing with excitement.

He had wild visions in his head. They were demented, power-mad. He saw himself transformed into the grey wolf. Running with the white wolf, his pack leader, terrorizing the city. Bringing it to its knees. They'd grow whole fields of lycanthropous flowers, create more werewolves. Together those werewolves would conquer the world.

The Prof climbed out of the truck. The alarm was still shrieking, faint but insistent.

"I'm going to check that skylight," he said. "It's where Scott got in before." Albert had secured it. But the Prof thought, *Whatever he's done, it won't be enough.* Eating lycanthropous flowers had made Scott into some kind of unstoppable maniac.

Thinking of this made the Prof look back at Ellis. But his ward seemed safely asleep, his head tucked into his arm, as harmless as a baby.

"He doesn't seem as badly affected as Scott," the Prof told Meriel, in a whisper so he didn't wake up his ward. "In fact, I think Ellis is recovering really well. Maybe he didn't eat as many flowers as Scott."

The Prof limped towards the skylight. Meriel slid out of her seat to follow him. Then she poked her head back in the truck.

"I know you're not asleep," she told Ellis. "And I know you're not recovering."

Ellis raised his head. Two fanatical golden eyes glared at Meriel. "Yes I am recovering," he said. "I'm totally cured."

"*Huh!*" said Meriel, with a scornful toss of her head that made her bone necklace rattle. "Who do you think you're kidding? You're talking to *me*, remember?"

Ellis snarled softly. "Keep out of my way," he told Meriel, baring his teeth.

But Meriel seemed totally unafraid. "I'm not going to let the werewolves have you," she said, defiantly. Then she darted away, quick as a dragonfly.

He saw her running off, in the glow of the car park's security lights. She disappeared, round the side of the building.

Now he was alone, Ellis burst into harsh, triumphant laughter. What did a small, skinny girl think she could do against the might of the werewolves? Even she and the Prof combined didn't stand a chance.

As Meriel raced towards the skylight, the alarm got louder, more manic.

She saw the Prof, kneeling, staring down into the basement.

"I can see Scott!" yelled the Prof, above the wailing siren. "Look, he's down there!"

Meriel squatted beside the Prof. She saw Scott sprawled face down on the white tiles of the refrigeration room.

"He looks dead," shouted Meriel, not sounding very sorry about it.

"We've got to get to him," the Prof shouted back.

"Okay," said Meriel.

She was gone before the Prof could stop her, leaping down through the skylight. He knew he couldn't follow her. It must have been a tight squeeze for Scott. But he'd never fit through.

The Prof stared down. He could see Meriel crouched over Scott. She lifted her face up, pushed aside her tangled hair, mouthed words at the Prof.

"I can't hear!" boomed the Prof. "Turn off the alarm! Turn it off! There's a switch! A switch on the wall!" He mimed flicking off a switch with his hands.

Meriel must have understood because she disappeared, briefly. Then seconds later, the alarm stopped.

In the silence that followed, Meriel declared, "He still looks dead."

"I'm coming down there!" the Prof shouted.

He'd have to take the long way round, through his apartment, then through the Dinosaur Hall and the basement corridors to reach the refrigeration room.

He hauled himself off his knees, already searching in his pocket for the key to his back door. He was hurrying, as fast as his lame leg would allow.

His mind was racing, working out his next move. Getting to the refrigeration room was urgent. But there was one thing he had to do first.

I'm going to go to my study, decided the Prof, *to destroy that lycanthropous plant. Before it causes any more deaths.*

He didn't need to go back through the car park to reach his apartment. So he didn't know that his ward wasn't still peacefully sleeping. That the museum truck was empty and Ellis was nowhere to be seen.

CHAPTER FOURTEEN

Ellis loped along a gravel path, through the museum garden. His eyes blazed with a fierce, burning hunger. There was only one purpose in his brain – to get to the Prof's study, eat a lycanthropous flower and become the grey wolf again.

He'd got a key to the Prof's apartment somewhere in his pockets. But he didn't try to find it. With a rock, Ellis smashed his bedroom window and climbed through. He padded across his bedroom and out into the hallway.

He was moving on, to the Prof's study, when something caught his eye.

It was a sign on his bedroom door that said, *PRIVATE. KEEP OUT!* Underneath he'd scrawled, *This means you, Meriel!* But Meriel never took the slightest notice of that. She was always busting in uninvited. No one, not even Ellis, told Meriel where she could and couldn't go.

Ellis paused by the sign. Something seemed to stir in his brain. A memory maybe of the boy he'd once been, the people he'd once cared for. For a split second, his face clouded with doubt. But then he caught another whiff of that musky wolf scent. The flowers were luring him, like a helpless moth to a flame. He growled softly and hurried on.

He padded into the Prof's study. He didn't need to switch on the light. Moonlight was spilling through the window, making dancing shapes on the walls. And there on the window sill was the last lycanthropous plant in the world. It had grown taller, bushier, as if to make up for the loss of all the others. White blooms covered it, like sinister blood-filled stars.

Suddenly Ellis felt calm, as if he knew his destiny. There were no stirrings in his brain any more, not a single doubt.

He left his clothes in a neat little heap. He stretched out an eager shaking hand, plucked a flower, crammed it into his mouth, gulped it down.

The transformation started almost instantly. It seemed to rip his body apart like a bomb blast. For a few minutes nothing existed for Ellis but pain.

That's when the Prof arrived. He stopped in the doorway, frozen with shock.

"Ellis?" he whispered.

He saw his ward's fur-covered body on all fours, already in wolf form. But Ellis's face was still changing. The Prof stared, horrified, as his ward's features were twisted grotesquely, then rearranged into a snarling wolf head. Before the Prof's shattered brain could grasp what had happened, there was a large grey wolf in his study.

"That can't be Ellis," murmured the Prof, desperately trying to deny what he'd just seen.

Then he saw the python-skin band just above the wolf's left foot. Two years ago, the Prof had flown out to Africa to fetch Ellis after the death of his parents. Ellis had disappeared into the bush to grieve. He'd staggered out after two weeks, filthy, starving, his clothes in rags. But he'd still been wearing that wristband. The Prof had never known him take it off.

The sight of that band, more than anything else, seemed to snap the Prof out of his daze. He had to get his brain working, think of a way to get Ellis back.

The young grey wolf hadn't seemed aware of his presence. But then it slowly turned its head towards him, checking him out with its chilling wolf glare, its lips peeled back, showing its cruel fangs.

The Prof said, "Ellis?" again, as if he hoped somehow they could still communicate.

But the grey wolf growled, low and menacing. It didn't want to communicate with humans. It wanted to attack.

The Prof backed very slowly out of his study, not making any sudden moves. Then he told himself, *Run!* He had to get down to the basement.

He limped hurriedly down the hallway, past the huge round window. Through its stained glass, he could dimly see the Dinosaur Hall. The door that would take him there was only a few steps away.

He paused for a second, looked back. The grey wolf was loping behind him on long, rangy legs. Its eyes were fixed on him in that savage wolf stare.

The Prof fumbled for the bunch of keys in his pocket, frantically found the right one. He unlocked the door, dived through and locked it again behind him.

The Prof slumped against the wall until his heart stopped pounding. Then started out across the Dinosaur Hall.

He passed the massive scaly feet of the model *T. rex*, each with three deadly clawed toes. The *T. rex* was six metres high, looming above him, its great head lost in the shadows of the roof.

But the Prof didn't even notice it. He was frantic with worry. Meriel was with Scott's dead body, down in the basement. Ellis was the grey wolf – the Prof's brain still couldn't cope with that.

"Deal with it," the Prof ordered himself grimly. "It happened! You saw him change, right in front of you!"

Suddenly he felt the hairs rise at the back of his neck. He spun round, gazed at the round stained-glass window behind him. He could see the dark silhouette of the grey wolf on the other side, trapped in his apartment. It was prowling up and down. It stopped to stare through into the Dinosaur Hall. Even through the ruby-red glass, the Prof could see the gleam of its golden eyes.

Then the silhouette disappeared.

Where's it gone? thought the Prof, uneasily.

The window exploded. A dark shape burst through, as if it was rocket-powered, in one spectacular bound. A blizzard of red and blue glass flew glittering through the air.

The Prof ducked behind the giant leg of the *T. rex*, covered his head. When he looked up again, the grey wolf was loping towards him through the heaps of broken glass.

The Prof thought desperately, *It's indestructible!*

The Dinosaur Hall was a vast space, big as a cathedral. And the basement door was at the other end. The Prof knew he couldn't reach it before the grey wolf got him, not with his lame leg. Besides, he had to have time to punch in his security number.

His hand twitched on the plastic skin of the

T. rex's leg. He gazed up at the great, prehistoric beast.

Then his gaze switched to the grey wolf, padding towards him, murder in its eyes.

Suddenly the Prof told himself, *Fool!* He'd clean forgotten. The *T. rex* was animatronic – a moving, roaring model. Maybe he could use it to distract the wolf.

Where's the button? thought the Prof, frantically. It was right next to his hand, on the barrier that surrounded the *T. rex* to keep people from getting too close.

He pressed the button. Immediately, there was movement up in the gloom, a whirring and clicking of machinery. Suddenly, a huge scaly head came swooping down, its tiny red eyes lit up like twin fires. It swung to and fro, as if searching for prey. Its lizard tail thrashed about. One blow from that could knock over a bus.

Then it opened its massive, cavelike jaws, edged with rows of wicked teeth. It gave a thunderous roar. The primitive sound rumbled through the empty hall, like a challenge.

Its fighting instincts roused, the grey wolf leaped

the barrier. It sprang on the *T. rex*'s neck, clawed its way up to its head. Machinery whirred again and the model *T. rex* began rearing up. The grey wolf looked tiny, clinging onto its head. But it didn't care about the size difference, didn't care either that it was being carried up to the ceiling. Its attack was ferocious. It tore at the plastic skin of the *T. rex*'s head, ripped it to shreds. The roars were still coming, but you could see the dinosaur's shiny steel skull, and all the motors and wiring inside it. The grey wolf's strong teeth crunched metal. The *T. rex* began to malfunction. Its red eyes flickered on and off. Its head jerked, crazily.

The Prof stared at the bizarre battle going on above him, werewolf versus machine. The *T. rex*'s roars faded away. It shuddered to a halt, back in its starting position, its head six metres above the floor, its glowing eyes switched off.

The grey wolf stared down, still not scared, but growling angrily. It was too far even for a werewolf to jump.

For the Prof, it was the perfect chance. The grey wolf was helpless up there. He should have left it stranded and escaped. But the grey wolf was Ellis.

His ward was in there somewhere, locked inside that snarling bundle of fury.

"I can't do it," murmured the Prof.

What if Ellis slipped? Surely even a werewolf couldn't survive that fall?

So the Prof pressed the *Start* button again. Machinery whirred, metal clanked. The model was still working – just. A silver skull with red flickering eyes came jerking down from the shadows. The wolf was riding on top of it. As it neared the floor, the wolf's growls grew louder.

The Prof moved then, as soon as he knew Ellis was safe.

He hobbled towards the basement door. Feverishly, he started punching in his security number, his hands slippery with sweat. Behind him, he heard claws clicking on the tiles.

The grey wolf had already jumped down.

It's coming after me, thought the Prof.

But now the basement door was open. He dived through, shoved it shut behind him with his shoulder. He collapsed against it, weak with shock at everything he'd just seen.

Then he heard a familiar voice.

"Where have you been?" demanded Meriel, who'd come to find him. "I've been waiting ages."

"Ellis is a werewolf," the Prof told her, in a dazed voice.

"Course he is," said Meriel, impatiently. "I thought you *knew* that. Oh, and by the way," she added, "that Scott guy, he's not dead. He's alive. He's waiting for you, in the refrigeration room."

CHAPTER FIFTEEN

When Meriel and the Prof reached the refrigeration room, Scott was huddled in a corner.

"We thought you were dead," said the Prof, astonished.

"I took wolfsbane," mumbled Scott.

"Wolfsbane!" said the Prof. "That's an insane thing to do! It's deadly poison!"

"I know," said Scott. "I don't know why I'm

still alive. And look..."

He held out his unbandaged hand to show them. His hand was smooth and pink again. There was no sign of fur at all. His long yellow wolf claws had shrunk back to human nails. He was pale, very pale, but his eyes had changed back to blue again and he'd stopped twitching and scratching his itchy skin.

"I think I'm cured," said Scott. "I'm not a werewolf any more."

The Prof stared at Scott suspiciously. Meriel's words, *Never trust a werewolf*, flashed through his mind. Perhaps this was just another clever trick.

Scott could see the Prof wasn't convinced. The trouble was, Scott was bewildered too. He had no idea how he'd survived and, it seemed, been totally cured.

But suddenly the Prof remembered what the prehistoric plant expert had told him. Wolfsbane was a very peculiar plant. It had the power to kill werewolves. In the past, terrified people had made sure that it did. They'd tipped their arrows with a lethal dose. But, if the dose wasn't big enough, and the werewolf survived, the curse was lifted. The werewolf was cured, for ever.

All this was according to legend. But, this time, the Prof didn't doubt it. So many things from the world of myth and legend had come true since the Tattooed Boy arrived at the museum.

"I don't know why I'm still alive," Scott murmured again.

Briefly the Prof explained. When he'd finished, he said, "I thought you'd know that about wolfsbane. You're the expert on wolf legends."

"I did know," said Scott. "But I forgot. I think I was crazy when I was a werewolf. It wasn't me, wasn't me at all."

"You can say that again!" said Meriel. "And you made Ellis a crazy werewolf too," she reminded Scott, her eyes flashing angrily. "What are you going to do about that?"

The Prof shot her a look, as if to say, *Don't start on him, Meriel!* Now wasn't the time to be menacing. They had to concentrate on their main problem, which was how to free Ellis from the shaman's magic.

But Scott's face looked tormented. "What did I

do, when I was the white wolf?" he asked Meriel. "I can remember some of it, doing terrible things—"

"We'll talk about that later," the Prof interrupted. "For now, Ellis is our *only* concern..."

Scott shook his head to chase away those nightmare flashbacks of his time as the white wolf. He fought hard to pull himself together. "Where is Ellis?" he asked.

"Still in the Dinosaur Hall," said the Prof. "At least I hope he is. He ate a flower from my study and transformed into the grey wolf. Right there, in front of me."

The Prof shuddered at the memory. He, too, felt he was struggling to stay sane when things around him were becoming crazier by the second.

"Didn't you destroy the lycanthropous plant?" asked Scott, appalled.

"I was on my way to do it," said the Prof, tight-lipped. "But Ellis got there before me."

Then Meriel spoke up. In her usual blunt way, she said what the Prof and Scott were both thinking, but didn't dare say.

"We'll have to give Ellis wolfsbane," she said.

"No!" said the Prof immediately. "If we get the

dose wrong it'll kill him." He suggested a different plan. "We'll simply destroy the plant. It's the last one on earth, isn't it?"

Scott nodded. "As far as I know."

"That's our answer then," said the Prof. "Ellis will change back at dawn. So we make sure we destroy the plant before tomorrow night. Then he can never become the grey wolf again."

Scott shook his head, sadly. "You don't understand. He won't be cured."

"Why not?" demanded the Prof, bewildered.

"He'll still be a slave to the shaman's magic," said Scott. "All he'll want to do is become the grey wolf again. According to the legends, he'll wander the world, like a lost soul, searching for another lycanthropous plant. He'll waste his whole life in a useless quest. You won't be able to stop him. You'll probably never see him again. And he'll still have all his werewolf symptoms, hairy hands, golden eyes and the rest. He'll be an outcast, a freak, until the end of his days."

The Prof looked aghast at this awful vision of Ellis's future. He turned to Meriel. "What's your opinion?" he asked her.

"Scott's right," declared Meriel, who knew all about being an outcast in human society. "Wolfsbane is the only way."

"No!" The Prof still couldn't bear to think about the risk. "And anyway, how do we get him to take it? He *definitely* won't take it in his grey wolf form. You've seen him," he appealed to Meriel. "He's so savage you can't get near him. He'll kill anyone who tries. And even during the day, in human form, he's cunning and super-strong."

"In the old days," Scott reminded the Prof, quietly, "they shot werewolves with wolfsbane. They smeared it over their arrowheads."

"Are you suggesting I shoot my own ward," said the Prof, outraged, "and with a deadly poison?"

"I'm only talking about a flesh wound," said Scott. "A slight cut. That's what I did." He unwrapped the towel from his injured hand and showed the Prof. "I made the wolfsbane into a paste with spit. Then I rubbed it into this cut. Once it got into my bloodstream, it worked really fast."

"No," said the Prof again, shaking his head. "I won't do it."

"You're a really good shot," Meriel pointed out.

"No!" insisted the Prof. "We don't know the right dose. It's far too dangerous. I won't be responsible for my own ward's death."

"He's worse than dead," said Scott grimly, "if we leave him the way he is. Being a werewolf is a sort of living death. I know that better than anyone."

"But you still haven't answered my question," said the Prof desperately. "How do we know the right dose?"

"We give him the dose I took," said Scott. "But a little bit less because he's lighter than me."

"*A little bit less!*" the Prof burst out. "That's hardly scientific. This is Ellis's *life* we're talking about."

The Prof had an agonizing decision to make.

You must *use the wolfsbane,* he told himself. *It's the only way to save Ellis.*

But then a grim voice in his head said, *What if you kill him, instead of curing him?* And the Prof was in mental torment all over again.

Meanwhile, Meriel had got tired of waiting. She'd dashed outside the refrigeration room. The Tattooed Boy's possessions lay on the lab bench. During the day, some boffin had restrung the

Tattooed Boy's bow. They'd taken the two fledged arrows out of the quiver.

"Looks like a good bow," said Meriel, approvingly. "And these arrows are sharp."

Then she saw some powder in a little glass box.

"This green stuff wolfsbane?" she called out.

Scott came running into the lab. "Put that down!" he said.

He didn't know that giving Meriel orders never worked. She ignored him, tipped it out onto the lab bench.

"Is this the right dose to cure Ellis?" she asked Scott.

"That's deadly poison!" said Scott. "Don't touch it."

"Is it the right dose?" demanded Meriel again.

Scott tried to think, make calculations in his head. But in the end he could only guess. "Not as much as that," he said. "That's enough for two arrowheads."

A sudden sound made Scott's head whip round. It came from the refrigeration room, where the Prof was standing beside the Tattooed Boy's chamber, his mind still in turmoil about what he should do.

"What was that?" said Scott.

The sound came again. It was a low, rumbling growl. Scott felt his blood chill.

"Wolf!" he whispered, his eyes wide with horror.

Meriel dashed to the refrigeration room. She could see the Prof inside gazing upwards. But before she could reach the blue door, the Prof hissed, "Get back!"

Meriel hesitated. The only person she took orders from, sometimes, was the Prof. She skidded to a stop in the doorway, peered upwards too, and saw the grey wolf staring down through the skylight. It had escaped, somehow, from the Dinosaur Hall. Its eyes gleamed with golden fire, its fangs were white and glistening. Another growl rumbled in its throat.

"Get back!" the Prof told her again. His took his eyes off the grey wolf for a second, looked round at Meriel. He could tell instantly from her face that she wasn't going to obey him. Reckless and headstrong as usual she was about to come rushing in. And now Scott was behind her.

The Prof checked the skylight again. The wolf

had its front paws on the edge. The crest of fur along its spine bristled. It got ready to spring, bunching powerful muscles under its sleek grey coat.

The Prof took a few careful side steps to the blue door, all the time staring upwards.

Meriel thought he was going to save himself. Scott thought the same. They were both wrong. Instead, the Prof pushed Meriel back into the lab and slammed the blue door. Meriel rattled the handle desperately. "Prof!" But it wouldn't open. The Prof had locked it from the inside.

There was a small frosted glass panel in the top of the door. Meriel pressed her face to it. She could only see blurred shapes. Something came hurtling down from the skylight.

"The grey wolf's attacking the Prof!" said Meriel.

She ran back to the wolfsbane, spat into it, mixed it to a paste with an arrow point.

"Break the glass!" she cried to Scott. "Break the glass in the door."

"I'll fire the arrow," Scott said.

"No," said Meriel. "I'll do it."

She used the wolfsbane paste to coat the two

arrows, stirring them around in the sticky green mess.

Scott knew he should take charge, insist again, "I'll fire the arrow." But there was something about Meriel's feral stare that froze the words in his throat. It seemed to say, *Back off! This is my business!* The only two people she really cared about were both in that room. Scott guessed he'd have to fight to get the bow from her. And she'd fight like a wild animal.

They could hear ferocious growls from beyond the blue door, metal clashing as if steel trolleys were being toppled. Desperately, Scott grabbed the Tattooed Boy's axe, still stained red from where it had gashed his palm. He swung it at the frosted glass panel. The panel cracked and splintered. Scott punched out the broken glass with his bandaged hand.

Meriel gave Scott one arrow. "Here, hold that."

Scott held it by the flight feathers, well away from the poisoned tip. Meriel fitted the other arrow in the Tattooed Boy's bow. She peered in through the hole in the door. The Prof was cornered, trying to fight off the lone wolf. He grabbed a steel trolley, sent it skittering towards the grey wolf on squeaky wheels.

The grey wolf sprang over it, in one graceful flying leap. The trolley clashed into the wall behind it. Now there was nothing between it and the Prof. It flattened its ears against its head, growled viciously, padded forwards a few steps.

Meriel fitted her arrow, pulled back the string, aimed with one eye squeezed shut.

As the wolf crouched to attack, it raised its ears. They were large, meant to catch howls from kilometres away. It was what Meriel had been waiting for. An ear wound wouldn't do much damage.

She loosed her arrow. It missed and went whistling over the wolf's head, clattered off the Tattooed Boy's refrigeration chamber. The wolf sprang again, straight at the Prof.

It knocked him flying.

Meriel snatched the other arrow from Scott.

The Prof was on the floor now, face down, his arms protecting his head. The grey wolf was standing on his back, tearing at his jacket.

Meriel fitted the last arrow in the bow. She hardly had time to aim. The arrow sizzled through the air.

Meriel thought, *I've hit the Prof!*

But it seemed something had guided her hand. The arrow stuck, quivering, into one of the wolf's big back paws.

The grey wolf growled, leaped off the Prof's back and twisted round, snapping at the arrow in its paw.

"What's happening?" said Scott.

"I hit it," said Meriel briefly, without turning round.

The Prof stayed very still while the grey wolf writhed and snarled, trying to get its fangs around the arrow. But its teeth were made to crush and tear – they couldn't get a grip on the narrow shaft. And the wolfsbane was doing its work. The grey wolf was weakening. It couldn't get up. Its claws scraping the tiles, it dragged itself over the floor. Meriel, peering through the hole in the door, couldn't see it now. It had crawled behind one of the trolleys. It was howling now, terrible heart-rending howls, as if it was dying.

Meriel was frantic. *Was the dose too much?* she thought. "Let me in!" she demanded, beating at the door with her fists.

The Prof ignored her. He staggered to his feet and went limping over to where the grey wolf was sprawled. He crouched down. Meriel couldn't see either of them now.

"What's going on? What's going on?" Scott was pleading behind her back.

"Let me in!" screamed Meriel, trying to kick the door down.

The grey wolf's howls rose to an agonizing crescendo that made Meriel turn away from her spyhole and cover her ears. She just couldn't bear to listen.

I've killed Ellis, she thought.

When she took her hands from her ears, there was silence. The howls had stopped. The only sound you could hear was the quiet humming of the Tattooed Boy's refrigeration chamber. Trembling, Meriel looked again through the hole in the blue door.

The Prof was hobbling towards the door. Meriel had never been much good at reading human faces.

She couldn't read the Prof's now. Was Ellis dead or alive?

The Prof unlocked the door, swung it open. "You can come in now," he told Meriel.

She went darting in.

A body was lying on the tiles, covered in a white lab coat.

"Ellis!" said Meriel, rushing over, squatting down beside him.

He'd transformed from the grey wolf. All his werewolf symptoms had gone. He looked like Ellis again, but deathly pale and his eyes were closed. One arm, the one with the python wristband on it, flopped from under the lab coat. One foot poked out, with a wound, where the arrow had gone in.

"Ellis! Wake up! Wake up!" screamed Meriel, shaking him angrily.

The Prof pulled her away. "Take deep breaths," he told his ward.

Meriel took great panting breaths like a dog, calmed herself down.

"Ellis is alive," said the Prof, trying to keep his voice steady. "He's alive and I think he's going to be okay. Do you understand?"

Meriel nodded dumbly.

Suddenly a voice came from the door. It was Scott. They'd both forgotten about him.

"There's one last thing to do to end all this," Scott told the Prof. "You must destroy that lycanthropous plant in your study."

"That's the first thing I'm going to do," said the Prof. "After we get Ellis back to my apartment and put him to bed."

CHAPTER SIXTEEN

A couple of hours later, the Prof was standing alone in his study. Scott had left, on some errand of his own. Meriel was pacing restlessly around Ellis's bedroom, waiting for him to wake up. This was the first chance the Prof had got to destroy the lycanthropous plant.

That would put an end to this werewolf business once and for all. The Prof couldn't wait. This mission had stretched them all to the limit. It had almost wiped out him and his team.

And it was all because of that malevolent prehistoric plant.

What's the best way to destroy it? thought the Prof. He didn't want any of it to remain. Not a trace, not an atom. He didn't want any more werewolves in the world, ever.

I could do what I did before, thought the Prof. Stuff the plant into his kitchen blender and whizz it into a green goo, swirl it down the drain.

While he was thinking, the Prof took the plant off his study window sill. There was at least an hour to go before dawn and even more flowers had come out in a sinister display of power.

Their musky wolf scent filled the room. The Prof couldn't help breathing it in. And suddenly he felt his head swimming. He swayed, put a hand to his head. Pictures came slamming into his brain. He was running with wolves, wild and free, across endless plains. He was pack leader, howling defiance at the moon. He was invincible, lord of all creatures.

His fingers touched a fang-shaped petal, took

hold of a furry stem. A wolfish smile began to form on his lips...

Suddenly, someone snatched the plant from his grasp. The Prof whirled round angrily, ready to attack.

"It's me!" said Ellis. "Prof, it's me!"

The Prof stumbled, shook his head frantically, as if to scatter all those visions. He stared at his ward.

"What happened?" he said, dazed. Then he said, "Shouldn't you be in bed?"

"Good job I wasn't," said Ellis. "You were just about to eat a lycanthropous flower."

"I wasn't, was I?" said the Prof. He stared at the flowers in horror and disbelief. "Was I *really* going to do that?"

"It's not your fault," Ellis told him. "It's very hard to stop yourself. I couldn't."

Ellis clamped his mouth shut. He didn't want to talk any more about being the grey wolf. Luckily, he couldn't remember much of it. And what he could remember he hoped to forget soon. Like a really bad nightmare that leaves you traumatized, but gradually fades with time.

Ellis held the plant pot behind his back, as if he was scared the Prof might still be tempted.

"It's all right," the Prof assured him. "You can relax. I'm back in control now." He looked at his ward with concern. "But how are you feeling, after all you've been through? Will you be all right?"

Ellis thought about that. "I'm all right," he said finally. "A bit shaky. And my foot hurts. But, yeah, I'll be okay." He paused a second, then added, "It didn't help."

"What didn't help?" asked the Prof.

"Being a wolf didn't make the pain any better." Ellis didn't have to explain. The Prof knew he was talking about his dead parents. "It just made me angrier," said Ellis. "Much, much angrier. I hated everybody, even you and Meriel. I wanted to destroy the whole world."

"Let's get rid of this plant," said the Prof. "It makes good people into monsters."

Ellis nodded vehemently. "We've got to wipe it off the face of the earth!"

It was only a plant – it should be easy to destroy. But it seemed to Ellis that, like werewolves, it was cunning and powerful. If they gave it the slightest chance, it would find a way to survive.

As if he was reading his ward's mind, the Prof said, "I was wondering about the best way to destroy it."

"Maybe Meriel could eat it," said Ellis.

The Prof looked doubtful.

Then Ellis remembered. "Forget that," he said. "She's gone walkabout. She might not come back for hours."

"And we need to destroy it now," said the Prof. "As soon as possible."

Ellis thought for about five seconds. Then he said, "I know another way. And we can do it right now. This minute. I'll show you."

Ellis led the way, clutching the lycanthropous plant tightly, like a wild animal that might escape.

The Natural History Museum was one-hundred-and-seventy years old. It had seven floors of rooms, a maze of cellars and basements, and lots of forgotten and secret corners. Ellis, like a good tracker should, knew every metre of it. He guided the Prof down flights of narrow stone steps and stopped before a small wooden door.

The little label on the door said, *Boiler Room.*

"This is where Albert hangs out," said Ellis.

"I've never been down here before," the Prof confessed.

"I come down here often," said Ellis, "rat tracking."

Rats loved the warmth of the boiler room. Whenever Albert found rat signs, he'd summon Ellis. Ellis would track the rat's teeth marks, and the greasy smears left by its fur. Then he'd block up whichever tiny hole it had used to squeeze in from outside.

"But the room's locked," said the Prof, trying the handle.

"I know," said Ellis. "Albert doesn't start work until eight o'clock. But he leaves a spare key."

Ellis lifted the small rubber mat by the door. Under it was an iron key. He unlocked the door, and ducked to get inside.

"Welcome to Albert's den," he told the Prof.

Immediately the Prof was hit by stifling heat. All around him was hissing and gurgling. The boiler room was like a vast gloomy cave. There were huge pipes snaking off into the dark.

Set in the brick wall, at about Ellis's head height,

was a heavy iron door. It was round, and black with age. It had curly ironwork hinges and a big iron wheel to open it. The Prof heard a faint growling noise, like some kind of wild beast was caged up behind it. Then he caught a whiff of the plant again. "Whatever you're going to do, do it quickly," said the Prof.

Ellis put down the plant pot, then pulled on Albert's fireproof gloves. Using both hands, he hauled the iron wheel clockwise. The door swung slowly open. The growl became a crackling roar. A glowing red fireball seemed to leap out at them. Ellis shrank back. The fierce heat almost blistered his eyeballs.

"The furnace," he told the Prof. "Alfred says it dates back to Victorian times. It heats the whole building."

The Prof stared, mesmerized, into the heart of the flames. For a moment, he even forgot the plant's heady scent.

Then Ellis said, "Will you throw it in, or shall I?"

The Prof shook himself, remembered why they were down here. He stared at the lycanthropous plant. The flowers had been thickly clustered before.

But now, as he watched, they were shrivelling and dying. That musky smell was fading. And no new buds were forming – as if the plant had already given up, as if it knew what was coming. But then the Prof noticed something. On one stem, a fat grey pod was swelling.

Ellis had seen it too. "That's not a bud, is it?" he asked. "It looks different."

"It's a seed head!" said the Prof, horrified. "It's got seeds inside. And each of them can grow a whole new plant! We're destroying it just in time."

"Then let's do it!" said Ellis, suddenly frantic, as if he feared that the longer they waited, the more chance the plant would have of, somehow, fighting back.

"You do the honours," said the Prof.

Ellis grabbed the plant. Shielding his eyes, he hurled it into the furnace. There was a brilliant white flash, a shower of sparks, and the plant was incinerated.

"That was easy," said Ellis, his voice a mixture of relief and doubt.

"Even a lycanthropous plant can't survive that," the Prof reassured him. "It's over."

Ellis closed the furnace door.

"So where is Meriel?" the Prof asked Ellis, as they climbed back upstairs to the apartment. "I left her with you, in your bedroom."

Ellis grinned. "You know how she hates being cooped up. She was nearly climbing the walls! I told her she needn't stay. So she shot off, out the window. Who knows where she is now?"

Meriel had gone back to the wolf enclosure, to the clearing below the ridge, the pack's usual night-time place.

When she slipped out of the trees, she saw Nathan fast asleep among the wolves on the mossy ground.

Star, Grey and Dancer welcomed her, sniffing and nuzzling, like she was one of them.

Storm stayed aloof, like a pack leader should. He was sprawled, resting, on the highest rock, where he could see all around. Meriel grinned. She could see he was in charge again. Grey and Dancer raced madly about, wrestling and snapping in a play fight. They rolled too close to Storm's rock.

He gave them a warning growl, just to remind them he was boss.

Meriel sat hugging her knees, watching the sun rise, flooding the sky with pink light.

The cubs came rushing out from their den and jumped all over Nathan, using him like a bouncy castle.

He woke up.

"Hi," he greeted Meriel, sleepily. He didn't seem at all surprised to see her there. "Were you mind-reading the wolves?" he asked her.

"No." Meriel shook her head. She didn't need to. She could see by just looking that the pack was relaxed, back to normal. As if they knew there was no threat any more from wolf men.

"I know what happened last night at the Natural History Museum," said Nathan. "That Scott got cured. He's not a werewolf any more. And Ellis got cured too."

Meriel nodded. She didn't mention her part in the affair, how she'd shot Ellis with the poisoned arrow. Meriel lived in the here and now. As far as she was concerned, last night was over and done with, in the past.

She just said, "How do you know about Ellis?"

"I was passing the Wolf Camp office," said Nathan, "on my way down to the enclosure. And I heard the phone ringing, so I went in and picked it up. And it was Scott. He was at the hospital with Wolf Man. Scott told me what happened. I was still mad with him, 'cos he nearly killed Wolf Man, didn't he? And I thought Scott would be mad with me, like say, 'You're not allowed at Wolf Camp!' But he didn't. He said, 'You can stay. Wolf Man trusts you, so that's fine by me.' And then Wolf Man spoke to me."

"Wolf Man?" said Meriel, surprised.

"Yeah!" said Nathan. "He's woken up and he's okay. He says he's coming home tomorrow. He says there's a job for me here if I want it, working with the wolves."

"Do you want it?" asked Meriel.

"Might as well." Nathan shrugged, trying to sound as if he wasn't bothered. But his pinched, half-starved face betrayed him. He looked joyous, as if he could see a whole new life opening up for him. Something he thought would never happen.

"Well, don't mess it up," Meriel warned him,

in her usual blunt way. "Don't be an idiot. Do what Wolf Man tells you."

"Course I will!" said Nathan, indignantly. "Wolf Man's the Man!"

"I don't do what anyone tells me," said Meriel cheerfully. She sprang up. "See you later!" But suddenly, she hesitated a second.

She tugged her necklace of bones over her head and draped it around Nathan's neck.

Nathan's first thought was, *What's she done that for?* Then he realized he'd been given a gift.

"*Er*, thanks," he said awkwardly.

"Stoat vertebrae," announced Meriel. "I like stoats. But weasels are my absolute favourite."

Then she was dashing off again.

"Where you going?" Nathan shouted after her.

Meriel was running for the wood, fast as a hare. She paused and gazed at the dawn sky. It was streaked now, with bands of red. There was a raven in the distance, flying high, feathers glittering in the fiery glow. It was swooping this way.

Meriel yelled back an answer to Nathan, before she vanished into the trees.

"I'm going flying!" she told him.

CHAPTER SEVENTEEN

A week later, Ellis and the Prof were up on the roof of the Natural History Museum. They were watching a helicopter take off. It created a mini whirlwind as its rotors thudded round.

The copter was carrying an orange body bag. Inside the bag was the Tattooed Boy, packed in layers of ice. He was being airlifted to another museum. A prehistoric boy, found with all his possessions, was an exciting discovery. Scientists all over the world wanted to study him.

The rotors were whizzing around now. The copter rose into the sky and swooped away over the city.

"Bye, bye, Tattooed Boy," said Ellis.

Meriel wasn't here to see the Tattooed Boy's departure. He'd never meant much to her. She was off on some business of her own, with Travis draped around her neck like a red scarf.

But Ellis would never forget the brave warrior boy who'd stolen the shaman's magic and died because of it. Perhaps he'd been corrupted by it, like some legends said. But Ellis didn't blame him for that. He knew from bitter experience that the lycanthropous plants just couldn't be resisted. Even the Prof had been tempted.

The Prof said, "I've got something for you."

"Yeah?" said Ellis. "What is it?"

The Prof opened his hand. Coiled in his palm was the Tattooed Boy's thin plaited wristband. "I thought you should have it," the Prof told his ward. "They'd taken it off him. It would only have ended on display in some dusty glass case somewhere."

"But won't the boffins notice it's missing?" asked Ellis.

"Probably," the Prof grinned. "But I'll just look innocent."

"Thanks," said Ellis. He took the band gravely, slotted it onto his own wrist next to the python-skin band.

"It fits exactly," he said.

It didn't freak him out that it came from a dead body. He didn't remember the prehistoric boy like that. He remembered him as a living, breathing hero, with his red snaky dreadlocks, blue whorls tattooed into his skin and copper axe blade flashing in the sun.

The copter was just a dot in the distance now. Then it disappeared altogether.

"Come on," said the Prof, leading the way down from the roof. "I got a call today, another mission that might interest you and Meriel..."

Down in the boiler room, Albert, the museum caretaker, was tending the furnace. He was emptying the ashtray that was underneath it. Putting on his heatproof gloves, he pulled out the heavy, metal tray. It was full of heaps of ash from the coal that had burned in the furnace.

He didn't see that hidden in the ash were seven black seeds. They were shaped like tiny death stars. They had a scaly coating, as if protected by armour. No other seeds could have survived the white-hot flames of the furnace. But these seeds had.

Albert left the tray on the boiler room floor. When the ash was cold, he shuffled outside and threw it into the wheelie bin.

It was Wednesday before a garbage truck came to empty the bin. The truck dumped the rubbish it had collected at the vast council tip outside the city, where clouds of seagulls screamed and bulldozers clanked around, flattening the trash mountains.

At five o'clock the tip closed for the day. Darkness fell. The trash mountains lay quiet and still in the moonlight.

On the slopes of one of them, a tiny fist punched up though the trash. It unclenched into a leaf. Fast as a speeded-up film, more shoots burst through, their leaves grey and furry. Followed by a single, fat flower bud.

Animal Investigators: Wolf Man
FACT FILE

OTZI THE ICE MAN

- A Stone Age body was found in a glacier in the mountains by hikers in 1991. Scientists named him Otzi after the Otzal Alps where he was found.
- Otzi had tattooed skin and was wearing a cloak, bearskin cap and fur leggings. He was also carrying a dagger, longbow, copper axe and a little pouch with plants and herbs inside.
- Otzi was found with an arrow in his back. What was he doing so high in the mountains? Who shot him? Who was he? Was he a healer, a trader, a warrior, a shaman? It's still a mystery.

WILD WOLVES AND PEOPLE

- It's thought that early humans and wolves worked together to survive – that wolves taught humans how to hunt in groups, and acted as lookouts and guards.
- The last wild wolf in Great Britain was shot in Scotland in 1769.
- Wild wolf packs have been successfully re-introduced into Yellowstone Park in the USA. Now some people want to do the same in the UK.

WOLF FACTS

- A pack leader is called the Alpha wolf.
- Wolves measure up to 1.8 metres, nose to tail, and can sprint at 35 miles per hour.
- The whole pack takes responsibility for raising the cubs – finding food, protecting them and teaching them how to hunt. Wolves have even been seen running at cubs with deer antlers in their mouths, to teach cubs how to avoid getting stabbed by angry stags when out hunting.

MEDIEVAL BELIEFS ABOUT WOLVES

- A wolf's stare was thought to cause blindness.
- Wolves sharpened their teeth before hunting.
- A dead wolf, buried at the entrance to a village, kept away other wolves.
- Plucking and eating a lycanthropous flower when the moon was full transformed the eater into a werewolf. These flowers are still thought to exist in the Balkan Peninsula.

Don't miss more incredible missions
from the

ANIMAL
INVESTIGATORS

A half-crazed boy has turned up at the Animal Investigators HQ, raving about an army of gulls taking over his town, led by the malevolent Red Eye. Expert tracker Ellis and animal-mind reader Meriel must find a way to stop this deadly menace from terrorizing the town's people – before the death toll starts to rise.

ISBN 9781409506904

GHOST DOGS

While investigating rumours of a haunted forest, Ellis sights a ghostly dog pack led by a strange feral boy. The air temperature plummets to lethal levels, and Ellis suspects that the boy wields some deadly supernatural power. Can the Animal Investigators stop him before more lives are put in danger?

ISBN 9781409506911

KILLER SPIDERS

Famous explorer Jack Nelson has shut himself inside an experimental eco dome. System reports state that everything is normal, yet in a message received by the Animal Investigators, Jack raves that he is being attacked by giant spiders... Ellis and Meriel must enter the dome and find a way to combat the terror within.

ISBN 9781409506928

FOR MORE FEARSOME FICTION,
CHECK OUT
WWW.FICTION.USBORNE.COM

S.P. GATES worked as a teacher in Africa and then in England before becoming a full-time writer. She has since had over one hundred books published and, among other prizes, has won the Sheffield Book Award twice and been commended for the Carnegie Medal.

S.P. Gates is married with a daughter and two sons, and lives in County Durham.